Praise for *Scott Adlerberg*
& *Graveyard Love*

"Another masterful, twisted tale from the troubled, fevered brain of Scott Adlerberg, who leads the reader through the dark and winding canyons of a functioning psychopath and makes his personal horror seem normal. Almost. Keep thinking "almost" and you may escape having to undergo intensive therapy after the read. And… maybe not. It's worth taking the chance."

— Les Edgerton, author of *The Rapist, The Bitch, The Genuine, Imitation, Plastic Kidnapping* and others.

"Dark as the inside of a sealed tomb, *Graveyard Love* is Scott Adlerberg doing what he does best—taking a deep dive into the far reaches of the human psyche, where he illuminates the twisted intersection between infatuation and obsession."

— Rob Hart, author of *New Yorked* and *City of Rose*

"The ghosts of Cornell Woolrich and Edgar Allan Poe haunt the pages of this atmospheric thriller. Voyeurism, obsession and death — Alfred Hitchcock would have loved it."

— Wallace Stroby, author of the Crissa Stone series

"Scott Adlerberg's *Graveyard Love* is an unholy mix of Dostoyevsky's unreliable narrator, Poe's macabre obsessiveness and Hitchcock's ratcheting paranoia and suspense. You don't want to miss this unpredictable tale of insane brinksmanship."

— Travis Richardson, author of *Keeping the Record* and *Lost in Clover*

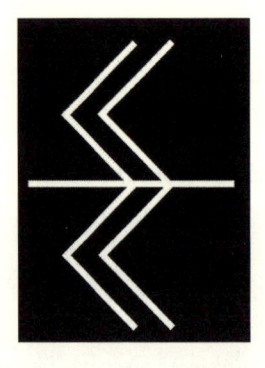

A Broken River Books original

Broken River Books
10660 SW Murdock St
#PF02
Tigard, OR 97224

Copyright © 2015 by Scott Adlerberg
Cover art and design copyright © 2015 by Matthew Revert
www.matthewrevert.com

Interior design by J David Osborne

All rights reserved. No part of this book may be reproduced or transmitted in any form or by any means, electronic or mechanical, including photocopying, recording, or by any information storage and retrieval system, without the written consent of the publisher, except where permitted by law.

This is a work of fiction. All names, characters, places, and incidents are the product of the author's imagination. Where the names of actual celebrities or corporate entities appear, they are used for fictional purposes and do not constitute assertions of fact. Any resemblance to real events or persons, living or dead, is coincidental.

ISBN: 978-1-940885-31-5

Printed in the USA.

GRAVEYARD LOVE

BY
SCOTT ADLERBERG

BROKEN RIVER BOOKS
PORTLAND, OR

PART ONE

ONE

On Sunday, though sober, I walked into the graveyard. I left the house and crossed the road and went over there. Snow had fallen Saturday night and I had on my hiking boots. The snow wasn't deep but coated everything, and beyond the expanse of vaults and tombstones, the trees in the woods glittered white. I'd dressed warm for my stakeout — black dungarees, a sweater, my fur-lined parka and red knit cap — but cold as it was, I felt terrific. I'd recovered from my hangover. Yesterday I'd drank nothing and today, so far, nothing either. The late afternoon skies were blue, the sun bright, the air calm. I loved this crisp wintry weather and would have gone out for a vigorous stroll, graveyard woman or not. By walking every day, I got my exercise and freshened my lungs. I removed myself from the cigarette stench my mother created with her Marlboro Mediums. She smoked two packs a day and since it was her house, I couldn't stop her. In my room only was her smoking off-limits. And my walk, besides, was a tonic for my nerves, a break from the pressures she applied. My mother and her book! Her goddamn memoir.

I was always inventing stories in my mind, plotting out novels and shorter tales. I promised myself that very soon I'd revive my own projects. My laptop contained lots of drafts and notes but I couldn't write my own things as long as I had my mother's book to do. Until that was dispensed with, I'd be buried in it, forced to give it my full attention. Anything less was unthinkable with my mother there breathing down my neck.

She'd dictate to me on most work days and sometimes she'd want to keep on paper exactly what she had dictated. Other times she'd prefer changes. "Punch it up," she'd say. Or: "Make it prettier." Or: "More artful. Embellish. You're the writer." But why she had me doing it, I couldn't understand. Her regard for me as a writer seemed low. I'd follow her directions as best I could, but she'd rarely be satisfied. She'd read the printed pages I gave her, snort, demand more changes with yet more instructions just as imprecise as her first ones had been. "Heighten the poignancy here," she'd say. "Here it should be funny but also serious." It was a hack's job. Ludicrous. And I'd think, *I must've been loco to take this on. How could I have? Time to quit.*

But that was my drudgery, the bind I'd let my life become, and this, being out in the graveyard to await the arrival of the red-haired woman, this was something new and mysterious. I could feel my heart racing. Despite the cold, my armpits were sweating. I thought, *my investigation, the beginning of my probe into this woman*, and saw myself as a detective:

Report in, Kurt.

Two or three times a week the subject comes to the cemetery and visits a grave.

Any idea why?

She's morbid.
Seriously.
Someone she loves has died.
But she never brings flowers.
Never brings anything.
You know which grave?
Not yet.
Continue with the stakeout.

The cemetery had an entrance, a swinging iron gate just off the road, and day or night, it was left open. I'd never seen it closed. A white shed stood inside the gate and here the attendants based themselves for their maintenance of the place. Some job they did: in summer wild grass and weeds would grow and not be cut for weeks on end. The bushes would be pruned intermittently and so give the graveyard a savage look. I liked it for that and others must have also because it was an active graveyard, with burials for locals occurring often. Not once had I heard of anyone complaining about the cemetery's upkeep, and since no church was attached to it, there seemed to be no religious requirements. Anyone could be buried here.

I planted myself in the doorway to a vault. From here I could see the road and my house. There it was, the white Victorian, overlooking the cemetery. If the dead were to rise, I thought, the first thing they'd see after the sky would be my house. In a zombie film they'd make a beeline for the house, and in that movie I'd be the guy who happens to look out his window and see them. They're shuffling across the road, a hoarde of gray-skinned, puckered beasts hungry for human flesh.

A high metal fence of pointy-topped posts surrounded the graveyard, so I set my watch on the entrance gate. The fence did have holes in it, but I thought the woman would come from the front, most likely in a car. Besides my mother and me, nobody lived nearby. Fields and woods dominated the area and the closest house was way down the road. The town itself was miles off. Beyond question, I thought, since moving from Brooklyn and joining my mother here upstate, I'd got myself caught in an unhealthy hermetic life, and despite my excitement over this stakeout, I felt a little ghoul-like slouching there among the headstones.

Sunday nobody worked in the shed. The graveyard was empty. Armed with a coffee-filled thermos, I settled in to wait in the vault, sitting down on its cold stone floor, leaning against a wall in the doorway. Bit by bit dusk gathered round me and the setting sun faded to gray. A whispering breeze sprung up from nowhere. I listened to it slicing through the woodland pines and I heard the harsh cries of blackbirds, perched in the naked trees of the graveyard. I was patient. I'd decided I'd wait till well after dark. I had my thermos of steaming black coffee and if I hadn't been doing this, I'd have been watching a movie in my room. Sunday night was horror movie night, and I'd either rent a couple of horror films or pick two to watch from my own collection. That's not to say that on no other night would I watch horror flicks, but Sunday was the night designated horror movie night, and I always looked forward to it for that reason. Two vampire movies or zombie films or classics starring Boris Karloff, or maybe I'd even have a triple bill centered around one director — Polanski, Argento, Bava. My worn blue recliner was a fixture in my life and there I'd sit with the door closed, the lights out, a candle lit. I'd watch the films while drinking wine and eating the dinner

I'd cooked for myself. That was my Sunday night, and the ritual I'd come to enjoy.

I waited till my coffee ran out, till long after sunset, when stars had emerged in the black sky, but the red-haired woman didn't come. The next night too she was a no-show and the night after that. Undaunted, I kept trying, crossing the road in the late afternoons, sitting in that vault in my cap, gloves and parka, but the graveyard woman did not appear. She never came walking through the entrance gate or any of the gaps in the fence.

A week went by.

Nothing.

The woman might've dropped off the face of the earth.

It was disheartening and I was wondering what to do. I'd sit in my room at night, in bed, and I would brood over her absence. Turned toward the window, I could see the graveyard, and I'd sit there in the dark sipping red wine. Without doubt it seemed foolish to continue with the stakeouts, and during the week, on some of the evenings, people had seen me in the cemetery. I'd had to move from the vault doorway and go stand over a grave as if I was paying someone my respects. To loiter in the vault with my thermos looked suspicious. So when a week had passed without any sighting of the graveyard woman, I threw up my hands and said forget it. She was somewhere else and I might not ever see her again. I'd be smart to put her out of my mind.

I went back to my customary habits, resumed my twilit hikes through the woods. When work on the memoir was done for the day, I'd bundle up in layers and go. But I had new questions. *Why* was the woman no longer visiting? For weeks she'd been coming two or three times a week, usually at dusk, always in her shiny black cloak. She had a fluid sliding gait and that dark red hair flowing down her back and I'd watch her from my window till she walked out of view among the vaults and tombstones. Naturally, I'd spin stories about her. She was a murderer in one, a remorseful killer dolefully coming to kneel down at her victim's grave. I saw her weeping at her victim's gravesite, apologizing for what she'd done. Or maybe it was a child she'd lost. The total devastation of that. But why didn't she ever bring flowers or anything else to put by the tombstone? Something had to be driving her visits, some sort of obsession, yet now, apparently, she'd ended them. Was she ill? Off on a trip? Had she died? It's typical of my luck, I thought. The moment I'd determined to reach out to her, to eject myself from my self-constructed cage, she'd evaporated. I'd finally resolved I would try to connect with another human being, but just then the void had claimed her. A black hole had swallowed her up.

In my mother's memoir, we'd gotten to the part where her parents were leaving their expat life in Morocco. Before that, in the early fifties, they'd lived in Paris. As a child, she'd drunk tea with artists, rich idle travelers and down at their heel failures. Her schooling was haphazard and the atmosphere around her tolerant. Things like pot use, racial-mixing, and homosexuality were not taboo for her parents. But when her parents returned to the States and opened a crafts and clothing shop selling North African items, she started high school in Manhattan and had to undergo an adjustment. She tried her best. Every now and then her mother would publish a photography book and her father would sell a painting. And it was this time, during her transition to American culture, to orthodox schooling, to a life more regulated than her airy existence abroad, that she was describing for me now. I'd be sitting at the desk in the study and she would pace in her white running shoes. She'd dictate while pacing. She kept her white hair pulled back firmly, tied in a short tail at her neck. Sharp-eyed, beak-nosed, thin-lipped, my mother had a birdlike face and she had a wispy body to match. No fat weighed her down, no cellulite. At times she'd pace the floor so quickly, it seemed as if her feet weren't touching the rug. She'd be telling a story, smoking her cigarette, and her head would bob on her slender shoulders. She would hold her right hand partially closed, with thumb and forefinger extended, jabbing the air as she spoke. A high-strung woman, in short, made worse by the cigarettes and her addiction to Italian espresso, and I thought that one day when she went out to the driveway to get the paper the boy delivered, a strong gust of wind might lift her off her feet. Carry her away and deposit her somewhere in the trees. She'd fit right in with the blackbirds, I'd think, the birds as severe-looking as her.

But our work, the method we used — it was laborious; she'd give me the raw material, the vignettes and minutia in bald form, and I would expand on that. I'd shape and enhance her memories. Her gripes would follow, as I've been saying, but when she wasn't dictating, I could be alone at least.

"With you in the room," I'd once told her, "I can't write. Let me write a section, then you can read it and I can re-write it and so forth. Any objections?"

To which she'd stalked off to go do her pottery.

Strange to say, but awhile ago she'd flipped for ceramics, and soon after buying this isolated house, she'd set up a workshop in the basement. It had everything: kiln, tools, potter's wheel. Her interest had begun with a pottery class she took down in the city, around the time she and my father separated, and it had grown on her ever since. She did it for herself, making her pieces and putting them in a room upstairs — the "pottery room" — and she could spend whole days at it. She had a sink, a fridge, and an espresso machine in the basement, and that's where she'd be most of the time when not in the study with me for her book.

So routine had overtaken again, and the memoir grew page upon page. I felt such a letdown from the disappearance of the graveyard woman that I didn't have the strength to quit on my mother. Days I spent writing, evenings walking. Nights I'd drink, read, and watch movies. *Still stuck*, I'd tell myself, ensconced in my blue chair, but I couldn't leave. Stepping back into the world scared me. It would mean facing loneliness, my old enemy. I'd be alone out there again, confronted by the shapelessness of life. My world now, inside this house chockablock full of Moroccan lamps and Arabian carpets and liquidy landscapes painted by my grandfather, I knew cold. And even though my mother could be abusive, I was inured to it. We did have an intimacy between us; after all, I was writing her book, sharing the secrets and passions of her life. Because of her I had a connection with somebody, and out in the world, going by my track record, I'd have nothing. In any case, I couldn't see myself with anyone. Of my past girlfriends, the few there were, Charlotte was a fluke, I'd tell myself, and Maria was a long time ago. I saw myself in a gray room out there, the solitary occupant of an apartment, a prototypical lonely guy who barhops night after night.

Here I had nature to enjoy and a spacious house to live in. I didn't get claustrophobic. And drinking alone was nothing shameful.

Right...

But if the graveyard woman comes, I'd think, *wouldn't that bring a hope of something?* I'd thought so earlier but not anymore. She'd vanished to the winds and I felt relief. What would I have done if she had come? Introduced myself? Attempted to make small talk? She'd have shaken her head and left the graveyard with me filed in her mind as a creep.

Don't come, I was thinking now. *Wherever you are, stay there.* Because with her reduced to a fantasy, I could imagine a wonderful meeting. I could see her smiling, tossing her red-haired head, staring at me with inquisitive eyes. I'd say something meaningful to her, and she'd melt for me. Reality could not live up to that.

TWO

But then, one night, she came. Just after I'd written her off, I saw her.

That morning it had snowed, and the air hung heavy and cold in the woods. I was walking back home after my ramble, and the early evening moon of silver and blue bathed everything in a crystalline light. The snow was compact and ankle-high and I loved the sound of it crunching underfoot. In my boots, gloves, and hat I felt warm and I'd pause here and there and roll a snowball, fling it off into space.

I was leaving the woods, entering a clearing, looking directly ahead at the graveyard, when I saw somebody move over there. Nothing to shout about, I thought, the place does get visitors, but I quickened my stride and then was running. For some reason, my gut reacted. A twinge knifed through me. I tore across the clearing and over to the fence that formed one rim of the graveyard, and there the feeling in my gut was validated.

The black cloak, the black gloves, the long uncovered red hair...

I stopped, short of breath.

She must have paid her respects already because she was walking out the gate. A white two-door was parked by the road. Hunched by the fence, I watched her from the rear and an angle, and I could hear her talking to herself. I couldn't make out the words. Then she got into the car and keyed the ignition, pulled out from the gravel, drove off down the road. She was gone and I'd seen her all of thirty seconds, but to know she was back, frequenting the graveyard, made my day.

That night, over our dinner, even my mother couldn't irritate me. She was bitching about the latest pages I'd printed and I cut her off by quacking like a duck.

Her eyes were gray steel.

"I'll look at them tomorrow," I said. "Tonight I'm in a good mood."

"You are, are you?"

"For once, yes."

"For once? Don't put your depression on me. What's made you so happy?"

"Something. It wouldn't interest you."

"It interests me to improve this section. That guy was my first boyfriend and you haven't described it well. You haven't conveyed what I felt for him."

"Tomorrow," I said. "Give me your notes."

"I will."

"I'm sure."

And tomorrow, I thought, I'd be back on the lookout, prepared to go up and talk to her. She might snarl with repugnance, but I'd have to try.

A storm ripped through during the night and I awoke to see heaps of snow on the ground. The road past the house was buried. Ploughs didn't clear it till late in the day, when the sky was dark, so I counted the woman out for that evening. Not to worry, she'd return, and I knew what I'd do. Rather than skulk around the graveyard, I'd zip up to my room each day before sundown and lay in bed with something to read. I could hear all the traffic through the window and any car that parked across the road. If one stopped, I'd look over there, see who it was. I had my coat, boots, and hat by my bedside.

For two consecutive evenings I sat there. I pored over back issues of *Video Watchdog* magazine, reading about cult horror movies, the vampire cinema of Jean Rollin. When darkness fell, I'd take my walk, an abbreviated one down the road. But on the third evening she did drive up, shutting off her car by the cemetery gate, and I wasted no time getting downstairs, though I had no idea what I would say.

From the work of the ploughs, the road lay bordered by piles of snow. It was high beside the woman's car but at a lower level in the graveyard, and through a window in the living room I watched her shut her door, consider the obstacle, and push forward, clambering over a hard-packed mound in her cloak and black leather boots. She was agile, didn't stumble or fall, and slid from view down the other side. Then she reappeared past the cemetery gate, trudging through snow shin high. She'd come to do whatever it was she did, and no snow on the ground, however deep, was going to stop her.

The cold outside was arctic but windless. As I crossed the road, I felt the skin on my face tightening. Smoke streamed from my nose and mouth, and the whiteness all around, even now at dusk, with the sun departing and the sky a gray slate, was dazzling to see. The fields nearby were smooth cake frosting, the woods beyond shimmered with icicles. In the city, I was thinking, it isn't like this.

I climbed a ridge of snow myself but cut left and avoided the cemetery gate. If I'd gone in, she'd have heard me and looked and I still couldn't think of what to say to her. I'd observe her first, I decided, and see what she did at this grave she visited. I wanted to watch her perform her ritual, if it was that, and then talk.

Outside the graveyard, step by careful step, I moved along the fence. In such utter quiet it seemed as if my every footfall resounded and I could hear myself breathing. Yet the woman, walking up the cemetery's central path between two rows of vaults and tombstones, never glanced to either right or left. To be safe, I kept myself several yards behind her. She'd have had to twist her head far around to catch sight of me. And we continued this way, two people alone, dots in the snow, till she pivoted right and into a vault. A plaster-white cube. She'd gone inside through an arched opening and I came to a halt with my hands on the fence.

In a metal flask I had Meyer's Rum, heating fuel against the cold. I took a slug and put the flask back in my pocket, waiting for her to leave the vault. Given time to examine it, I was struck by its plainness. Though about the size of a garden shack, it had no engraved words, no scrollwork, nothing, on its exterior. *Any significance there?* I wondered, and waited on, standing motionless against the fence. My eyes were watering, and the tip of my nose, my fingers in my gloves, my toes, began to hurt.

Go, I thought, *go in there. It's a public cemetery. You're allowed here. Tell her the truth, that you've been watching her, but try not to scare her...Be friendly...Be yourself...Do it already...*

But when I went, I received a shock. I walked along the fence, ducked through a hole and trotted straight over to the vault...nothing. Inside I found nothing. An empty chamber: black stone and cement. Burning on a slab of this stone was a candle, and by its light I could see enough. The woman wasn't there.

Unnerved, I took a nip from my flask.

The sky, by this time, was turning an inky black.

Stay or go? I asked myself, scratching my hand against my chin.

I resorted to another chug of rum.

Then, like one awaking from a trance, I told myself, *No!* Impossible. I couldn't believe in people passing through walls. I told myself to inspect the vault because if she was not inside this chamber, she must have left it by some means. A door or a passageway. There had to be one. And did this chamber fill the whole vault? From the outside the vault had appeared larger than the space this chamber alone took up. There might be another room in here.

The candle on the slab stood in a black glass holder, and I picked it up to poke around. I tread lightly in my rubber-soled boots, silent as a cat on the concrete floor. And just like that I found the spot, a door in the wall, a section of metal built on hinges, and I saw that it had a hole for a key.

I squatted and pressed my eye to the hole. Blackness. But at my ankles I could see faint light, and when I cupped my hand over the candle, I could tell the glow was from another source, illumination behind the door. I bent lower to make sure, still shading the candle, dimming its light, and confirmed that, yes, the glow at my feet was spilling out from beneath the door.

She was in there, in another room or chamber, doing something.

I put my ear to the door's cold metal. I listened for noises, my eyes closed. It was tempting to push, see if the door would swing open, and yet I also felt leery of the door being opened and the woman catching me there. What would I say then? But neither happened. I restrained myself from pushing and she didn't open the door and after a time I could hear a voice that might have been the woman talking. The voice was subdued. And she was groaning, the sound sad, though with a rising hoarse inflection. I didn't know what to make of it.

I laid the candle jar back on the stone, uncapped my flask, and swigged. Returned to the door in a kneeling position, my elbows on my knees. The groans went on with their fervent melancholy and then I heard an indication of movement, scraping noises, and a single loud thwack. It sounded like a cupboard or drawer had been shut.

My cue, I thought, and tiptoed away.

I waited outside in the dark, behind a neighboring vault. And the red-haired woman did come out, her walk a glide even in the snow. She was heading for the gate. I couldn't see her well in the moonless starlight, but her hair looked more mussed than before. Her cloak was rumpled. Something stopped me from springing out and going over to talk to her, and I stayed where I was till off by the gate I heard her car engine start.

A wind had whipped up, glazing my face. *Soon I have to get inside,* I thought. But I didn't budge. If frostbite crept in, I'd deal. Fuck it. What would frostbite do? Cause me pain? I felt stupid for not having spoken and wanted to feel some pain. Yet I also wanted to check something. To take another look inside that vault. Who was buried there anyhow? Was the grave the stone with the candle on it or behind the door in the second chamber?

Tingling, I ran back in. The candle was out and the vault pitch black. But in my coat I had my pocket flashlight, an accessory kept in that coat for my evening walks in the woods, and when I switched it on, I saw that the door to the second chamber was wide open. I aimed the beam at the black stone slab; nothing was there except the snuffed candle in the black glass holder. No words were carved, no symbols. Then I stepped through the open doorway and into the rear chamber and my flashlight beam lit on a coffin. White stone. A sarcophagus. I walked closer, holding the flashlight steady, cutting myself a slice of light, and I swept my gaze over the figures inscribed in the stone. There were letters and numbers. The numbers were dates — *June 15, 1969 to April 10, 2011* — the letters formed words, and the words included a name: *June Hazzard*. It seems dumb, but that surprised me. I had expected one thing but this was another.

A woman was buried here.

THREE

The next morning a whistling tea kettle awoke me. As I opened my eyes, I took in a sky unclouded and blue. The sun shone gleaming white. But the air must've been glacial because no snow was melting, just reflecting back the sun, and looking out the window hurt my eyes. I'd slept in fits and starts, disturbed by dreams, jumbled dreams I couldn't recall, and my bedside clock said ten-thirty. The boiling kettle was my mother's way of rousing me, telling me to rise so we could work.

I ate my breakfast and got to it. I was writing about young love, my mother's first boyfriend. But after last night I couldn't focus and gazed at the laptop screen without typing. My thoughts zeroed in on the square white tomb, the groaning sounds I'd heard coming from behind the vault door. I needed to hear them again to guess at what they might be. Sobbing? Wordless prayers? What did the red-haired woman do in that back room and had she been doing it since April, these last eight months? Whether June Hazzard had been her lover or a relative or a friend, this much I knew — watching her up to this point had created more questions about her than answers. Yet with that expanding sense of mystery, my eagerness to talk to her had diminished. Shrunk to nothing. For awhile anyhow, I wanted to maintain my invisibility. If I kept watching from the shadows, like I had last night, I was bound to get a better handle on her. I mean, to begin with, it'd be great to see her face.

She might be disfigured, a voice advised me. *She could be scarred or her features deformed.* That would be something ironic, I thought, and with my luck, not improbable. But then again strangeness was strangeness. She was a woman of intrigue, whether homely or magnificent, and I felt compelled to keep watching.

In the vault, crouched by the metal door, I did. This happened two nights later. The candle in the front room was lit, the door between the two chambers was shut, and the noises she made again confounded me. Call them groans or moans or husky grunts — I could not deny that I heard eroticism. Anguish too, muffled weeping, but the breathiness in her sighs, the desperation — that was lust. Unmistakably. Or was I imagining it? Projecting something onto her? Like last time, I burned to kick open that door and look. Catch her in the act of whatever she was doing. But I couldn't. Behind that door, in that white vault, she was absorbed in a private act, and to barge in on her would have been a violation. So I left again, ran over to the neighboring tomb for cover, and I stayed there till she had gone. She walked through the snow like a hypnotized person, her head up and her back straight.

Inside the tomb, all was dark. The door between the two chambers was open. But nothing seemed undone in the back room: the white sarcophagus was shut. I put my flashlight down on the floor and tried to move the stone coffin's lid, felt the ache of my muscles straining. The lid, flat and white, was too heavy — no chance of me moving it. I re-gripped the flashlight and stood lost in thought, the flashlight beam lighting my feet, and kept standing there till I was shivering. The cold had gotten to me. It seemed like I'd hit an impasse with the woman, unless I could muster up the nerve to approach her, and a weariness I couldn't explain made me feel sorrowful.

I walked back across the road and fixed myself a bath. Not until later, after dinner, when watching a Knicks game in my room, did I think about the footprints.

Tonight and my previous night in the vault, I must have left tracks in the snow. They would lead from a hole in the graveyard fence over to the vault and out again. But my red-haired woman hadn't seemed to notice them. She'd never stopped, looked at them, appeared ruffled. She always moved with her unhurried glide. And she would arrive at the graveyard at dusk and leave the white tomb after dark. There'd been no moon tonight and none two nights ago, so maybe she just hadn't seen the tracks. But I couldn't push it. If there was snow on the ground, I'd have to keep my distance from her.

The next day, too jumpy to write, I ended my session in the late morning. Though my mother, down in the basement doing her pottery, thought I was at it in the study, I clicked off my laptop and went driving. I drove over to Kingston, an hour's ride, and bought myself a telescope there, and when I got back to the house, I set it up by my window.

This is how I'll see her face, I was thinking. *She'll step out of the car, when there's still daylight, and I'll take a good look.*

I heard a purposeful cough at my door.

"Is that you, mom?"

I turned around.

"And where have you been?"

She was standing in my doorway in a clay-flecked smock, a cigarette jutting from her hand, and her thin lips were rigid with censure.

"I had to go out," I said. "Buy something."

"For the book? Research?"

"No."

"I was being facetious," my mother said.

"Charming."

"Enlighten me then. Fill me in."

"I bought this."

I pointed at the telescope.

"Kurt?"

"What?"

"You left without a word, did almost nothing today, to go buy *that*?"

"It's not a sweatshop, is it? I do have the right to take an afternoon off?"

"The right?"

"Uh-huh."

She took a drag on her cigarette.

"I asked you a question, mom."

"Don't be an ass. Sweatshop! You could've told me, though. I'm downstairs and I thought you were working, then I come up here and see you're gone."

"I wanted to get this."

"You could've left a note."

"I'll work tomorrow."

She drew another puff and exhaled the smoke toward the ceiling.

"Ma? The smoke?"

"I have to tell you something, Kurt. For about the last week, two weeks, you've been treading water. Your writing's been..."

"Not what you want? That's shocking."

"It's been shoddy. Your mind's not on the job."

"Can I have some privacy please? I said I'll work tomorrow."

"Fine. Tomorrow then. But..." She straightened a finger, poking the air.

"What?"

"When did your interest in astronomy start?"

"Since I came to live with you," I said, and made a jaw-clenched grin. "It helps me remember there are worlds beyond this one. Whole galaxies, believe it or not, that ain't got shit to do with your book."

The graveyard, the tomb, my mother's book, the new telescope — I had one hell of a personal cosmos. *Freak, freak, freak,* I thought, and felt my head buzzing with the word. I slammed my door and went to the window, stared out at the line of pinewood hills. They were a dark green and white under the late evening sky, and though I was hoping for rain tonight to wash away my graveyard footprints, I didn't expect anything. Not even sleet. No clouds were in the sky and stars were shining like yellow jewels.

To calm myself I needed medicine. I had some on hand, and for convenience, I stowed that medicine in my closet. I had glasses, a wine rack, and my corkscrew there, and as my own consulting doctor, I prescribed myself a hearty syrah. I was drinking it then propped up in bed, my back against the pillows and the wall, when I told myself that next I'd want to follow my redhead outside the graveyard. That would make sense, to find out where she lived and how she led her life. Who does she sleep with? I thought. Is there anyone? Male or female? Whoever it was, they'd be sharing her with a dead person. Whatever she did by herself in the tomb, in the chamber with the stone coffin, she had an attachment to the woman, the deceased, a lover's devotion to June Hazzard.

I dozed off after awhile and when I awoke my stomach was grumbling. My mother hadn't called me for dinner. Or maybe she had and I'd slept through it. Anyway, I was famished, and I'd woken up with an erection. I knew I'd been dreaming of the graveyard woman as one does know without recalling particulars, and as I was lying there on my back, something happened in my mind. Since ouldn't put a face to the graveyard woman, I visualized her with lustrous hair but with the face of another. I saw young skin bruised with the creases of ill health, smudged red lipstick, the bleary bloodshot eyes of a junky. I saw in my head the face of Charlotte, and she looked like a zombie in a horror film, half-dead, half-alive.

Down below, I wilted.

Serves you right, my inner voice told me. *You fucked her that night and split, leaving her comatose. She needed you and you dumped her... You don't deserve anyone after that.*

I buttoned my pants and leaped from bed. But now, nauseated, I'd lost my appetite. I couldn't sit still in the house, though, watching TV or reading a book, so I got myself dressed and went outside, warmed the car while the windshield defrosted. Then I took a drive along the back country roads, my course aimless, and I rolled my window down a notch to feel the skin-tickling air. The black of the night in these parts was palpable, even with the stars, and I felt light cruising through it. I put on music, a classical station, a Vivaldi piece. Something buoyant with strings and horns. I knew that I wouldn't be able to go back into the tomb and spy on her, not till the snow on the ground melted, and this bothered me because I wanted to hear her again, listen to her making those impassioned sounds. *They're sounds of lust*, I kept telling myself. *She's doing something sexual in there, maybe touching herself.* And that image, of her in the tomb, with her hands under her black cloak, between her legs, caressing herself, made me hard once again.

FOUR

I had a rough time the following day. Back at work on the book, I dried up fast. Or I should say that I never got going because I was too groggy to write. I'd driven home around dawn, cooked eggs and bacon for myself, and slept. But before I knew it, the tea kettle was shrieking again and I resigned myself to getting up. I showered, brewed a pot of coffee, and then sat down at my desk. After our exchange of yesterday, I didn't want to hear my mother's reproaches about my wandering concentration. I had nothing in me, though, and the caffeine didn't light any fires. My eyelids were drooping and my temples beat with a dull pain. And the sunlight slanting over my shoulder, coming through the window across the study, warming my back and upper arms, increased my drowsiness all the more. After two hours of struggle, I surrendered, shutting down my laptop, and I stretched out shoeless on the room's sofa.

The door to the study was closed, my mother down in the cellar, chipping away at her pottery. As I drifted off, my thoughts lingered on the painted woman of the night before, the fucking I'd done in her slovenly place.

My mother's voice woke me.

"How 'bout lunch, Kurt?"

She had on jeans and her clay-spattered smock and a cigarette was in her fingers.

I yawned, unsure of the time.

"How long was I out?"

"You're asking me? It's two now."

"Three hours."

"Feel better?"

"I needed sleep."

"Why don't we go out for lunch?"

The offer seemed genuine, and I heard no aggravation in her voice. She inhaled on her cigarette and blew out the smoke, eyes wide, looking down at me, and the subtlest of smiles crinkled her lips.

"Well? Are you hungry? It'll be my treat, Kurt."

"Is something going on here?"

"What do you mean?"

"You see me snoozing, not working, and you offer me lunch."

My mother tilted back her head and I realized that for a woman her age she had a pretty, unwrinkled neck. A swanlike neck.

"Kurt, you're as hard to get through to as your father was."

"What's he got to do with it? I'll go."

"Don't let me twist your arm."

"You're not," I said. "I'm hungry."

But my father, I thought, she'd brought him up, and as I was changing in my room, I wondered what had made her think of him. Neither of us ever mentioned him much. When he was killed, my mother had been about to divorce him, and the murder had robbed her of the satisfaction of taking him to court and putting him through the proverbial wringer. She'd arranged his funeral feeling conflicted. There'd been love there once, so she was grieving, but she also felt resentful. His departure ruined her plans. For her a vicious divorce proceeding would have been a grand catharsis, and she'd been wanting that for herself after enduring his infidelities. That she gained more money through his death meant little — she'd been spoiling for the fight itself.

We took her car and my mother drove. I hadn't been driving with her in months. It reminded me of my childhood days, my mother bringing me clothes shopping or on an excursion out of the city, out to Long Island and the beach in the summer. On this day, the sky was overcast, the sun concealed, and the music she'd found on the radio fit. As I looked out at the snow, I recognized the work of Sibelius, a symphony of his, something dark and stormy from Finland. And my mother didn't speak while it played, as if the blustery composition spoke loud and clear for her soul.

Oh brother, I thought, and cocked an eye at her. But her face was blank. Did she have an announcement to make? Want me off the book? If that was so, how would I feel? Liberated, free to restart my own projects, but not just that. Discarded also. I'd taken too much shit from my mother to be shunted aside by her. Honor required that I see her book through to completion. Then if it had success when published I would know who was responsible. Or was she thinking of something unrelated, like my absence from the house last night?

That most certainly would bug her. But I had to have an outlet, didn't I? *She's living with a grown man*, I thought, *a guy with no girlfriend, and I seldom go out. To her that's normal? I should do nothing but use my hand, jerk myself off, for sexual pleasure?*

The woman last night had been a pick-up in a bar. Happens everywhere. I'd be hard-pressed not to laugh if my mother got on me for this.

The restaurant she chose, out on the highway, commanded a view of hills and a valley. The waiter seated us in the back, alongside a wall-size window. Snow flurries were falling, and the sky to the west, over the snow-capped crests of the hills, was gunmetal gray mixed with patches of blue. La Villa Bianca was the name of the restaurant, and despite the weather, the lunchtime turnout was respectable.

"Anything to drink?"

The waiter had doughy red cheeks and a pasta stomach but he held himself nicely in his white collared shirt.

"Mom?"

"I'll have a glass of wine. You have chardonnay?"

"We do."

"I'll have that."

"And you, sir?"

"Something red."

"We have Chianti, Merlot, a Nero D'Avola--"

"The Nero D'Avola."

If we were having drinks here, I knew there'd be no further writing today.

Over the wine, after we'd ordered our food, my mother got to it. She'd invited me out so we could talk, she said, so we could clear up what was going on with me. Maybe I was stricken with burn-out and maybe I needed a vacation, but unless I could reignite myself, we'd make no headway with the book.

"Are you implying," I said, "that I was doing alright till now?"

She sucked in her lips. "You were doing the job."

"Anyone can *do* the job," I said. "If that's the criterion. What I want to know is whether my work's pleased you."

"Kurt..."

"Because mom, if you're that dissatisfied, go elsewhere. There are writers everyplace. Why should we drag this on any longer?"

She made the admission that to get someone else, a professional ghost, would set her back at this stage. A new writer, a person she didn't know — it could mean starting from scratch. And she said that she couldn't do it alone; she'd tried before I moved in, and had learned she wasn't a writer. She did need help and who better than me, her writer son, to assist.

Your son's the only person who'll take your crap, I thought. *That's the real reason you want me. Another ghostwriter, paid well or not, would walk out on you.*

But she had come clean with the crucial revelation, that she couldn't finish the book by herself. I felt like I had the upper hand now, the power between us.

"I'd hate to quit this late," I said. "But you gotta ease up sometimes with the criticisms."

"It's all to make it as good as possible. Call me a perfectionist."

"Try to be a reasonable perfectionist."

The waiter served our food, chicken scarpiello for her, veal parmigiana for me, then sprayed on fresh black pepper.

"Thanks for the lunch, mom," I said. "I haven't had Italian in awhile."

"You're welcome."

Out past the window, the snow flurries were a pinwheeling chaos. They swirled in the wind, obscuring the hills. The sight of the flakes lent a peacefulness to everything, and so did the sound of the knives and forks brushing against other diners' plates. Everyone seemed becalmed — voices were murmurs.

"Now about last night," I said nonchalantly. "I—"

"I don't want to hear about it."

"No, it's just that sometimes—"

"You're a man," she said. "You have needs."

"A man."

"I don't know that because you're my son?"

She put a wedge of chicken in her mouth, chewed, and nodded. My sex life, or lack thereof, wasn't something she wished to discuss — evidently.

Shit, I'm not my father, I thought. *Married, screwing around, deceitful to his wife...*

"Maybe I am burnt out," I said. "I could use a break."

"Take your time. Maybe we both need to step back."

"A few days to recharge?"

"How many do you need?"

"Need or want? Three?"

"Take four."

I fell speechless, thunderstruck by her sensible attitude. But I pondered a question as I raised my glass and drank my Nero D'Avola. Years ago I'd written the article about my father's murder. The *New Yorker* published it and I relished the praise it drew from people though it derived from a terrible incident. Did my mother want me to write her story because she was competing with him? She hadn't been planning to use me for her book at first. She only asked my help with it when I got laid off in New York and came up to live with her. Rent savings was my rationale for coming, and stuck in my novel, blocked, I was hoping the rural environment would serve to refresh my imagination. I didn't foresee myself getting entangled in her never-ending memoir. Yet that's what happened. I wound up shelving my story and concentrating on her book. *It's nuts,* I thought, but I also saw how everything fit. By using me as her ghostwriter, my mother could outdo my father. Both my mother and father had been criminal defense attorneys, he with his own practice, she as a Public Defender for Legal Aid, and even during the happier days of their marriage, they'd been competitive toward each other. Now perhaps she was thinking that she would beat him posthumously. For him I'd crafted an article, for her I'd do a book, and if the book came out well, it would have a longer shelf life than the article. That could be why she was so demanding. She was shooting for a memoir that would last, a literary monument to herself. I couldn't be sure with her, however, and to ask her that question might wreck the rapprochement we'd forged. I said nothing. Why rile her?

FIVE

Stuffed from our lunch, my mother and I skipped dinner that evening. With carte blanche for some R&R, I got myself dressed to head on out. The flurries had ceased since the afternoon, but the temperature had dropped to near zero. I felt it soon as I stepped out the door. As the TV weathermen were saying, winter was upon us before its official date, and I could but marvel at the graveyard woman's determination. Or was it insanity? To come so often to the cemetery, to do whatever she was doing in the tomb, and to do it in this cold — I preferred not to pass judgment on.

I heated the car up in the driveway, mapping out my fun for the night. Maybe a movie, I told myself, and then barhopping, but no wallowing in the mire. No drunken sex I'd just want to forget tomorrow. None of that, and I swore that I wouldn't spend the night mulling over the graveyard woman. But as I was driving away toward town, brights on, fiddling with the radio, I passed a car I recognized as hers. The white two-door, a sporty Nissan. I looked into my rearview mirror and saw her angle over to the shoulder, roll to a stop by the cemetery gate. It was dark out already and later than usual for her to visit. Had something somewhere eaten up her time? A job? A friend? I hadn't been expecting her today; later in the week, I'd thought, I'll see her. Yet here was my chance, my opportunity to follow her outside the graveyard. The movies could wait and so could barhopping. Why not try to learn some things about her now?

I made a U-turn and cut my lights. I backed into the driveway so I could sit and watch her car. I let the engine run and the radio play, the classical station, a Tchaikovsky piece, and I gave myself up to the poignant music, the mournful tones of the elegiac Russian.

Swan Lake? No, Sleeping Beauty. Peter's the man when you're sitting in the dark staring across the road at tombs, at headstones, at earth that gets watered with tears. I'm obsessed with a woman who's obsessed with a woman who's dead.

The snowfall of the day had washed the air, shined it if you will. The night was a translucent black. I had the lights on my car off and could see as far as the woods past the graveyard. But what was my mother up to? She was in the cellar, I assumed, molding her urns and vases, and I hoped very much that she stayed there. If she heard the car idling in the driveway, she might think something was wrong and come out to ask me what I was doing. To hear the car motor running might make her think I'd cracked altogether, that I'd rigged a tube from the exhaust pipe to the driver's window. And how *would* she react if I died? If I killed myself? If I her child got to the grave before she did? Some mothers lash their breasts when that happens, but would mine even cry? For her book she would, because I wouldn't be there to write it anymore.

Twenty or thirty minutes went by before my red-haired woman came out from the cemetery. The black cloak, the black boots, the black leather gloves — she had on the clothes she always wore and I thought she'd drive off in the direction she always took. But she didn't; she drove the other way, south, continuing the way she'd been going when she arrived at the graveyard. I'd never seen her leave and go in that direction, and, flustered, I jerked the gear shift into drive and stamped down on the gas. The car screeched forward and spun on an ice slick, and by the time I got it straightened out, I'd squandered precious seconds. The graveyard woman was well ahead of me, her taillights receding yellow specks in the dark.

No problemo, I thought. I didn't intend to follow too closely.

The radio announcer said, as I knew, that I'd been listening to Tchaikovsky. Next would come Brahms, his second symphony. "Yuck," I said, and flicked the radio off. Brahms puts me to sleep. He always has. He's too — what's the word? — balanced. But play Wagner or Mahler, *crazies* with genius, and I'm enraptured. So I drove on in silence, maintaining a distance from the two yellow ovals, past the flat fields of snow. Then the ovals were gone, had moved right and vanished, and I slowed down as I neared some building lights by the road. *That's* where she was going: the Fieldhouse Tavern. A watering hole I patronized, it had once been a small farmhouse and outside it kept that look with its weathered planking and gabled roof. Did she come here much? That couldn't be. I drove straight so as not to park in the lot while she was there, but as I went past I took a glance over and saw her getting out of her car. Still in the black cloak, the hood down, red hair loose. She closed her door and then I swung my eyes to the road again, the dotted white line.

About eight people were sitting in the bar, and she was the only woman. She'd taken a stool far down the row, past everyone else, and when I walked in, the bartender was serving her. Something on ice in a whiskey glass, yellowish orange. She drank it through a thin white straw and the bartender uncrumpled her money, rang it up, returned with her change.

"Thanks C — "

Because of the music twanging, the country western tripe on the jukebox, I hadn't caught her name, but I figured I wouldn't be out of line if I asked Tony.

"Rum and Coke, Kurt?"

"Myer's, with a lime."

"You got it."

I watched him prepare my drink, bustling about in a plaid shirt and a black cowboy hat. He had a soft stomach, a chubby face, and the jaundiced complexion of an alcoholic.

"Thanks, Tony."

He was taking the twenty I'd laid on the bar.

"Let me ask you something."

"Yeah?"

"That woman. Who just came in. She isn't a regular?"

"Catherine? She comes in sometimes."

"Often?"

"Every so often," Tony said. "Why?"

"Just askin'."

Tony smiled, flashing yellowed teeth.

"You'll never see her sitting here with anyone. Ever."

"She must sometimes."

"Never," Tony said.

"And...why's that?"

Tony shrugged. "She won't accept a drink from you either if you offer."

"Boy!"

"Try it and see."

"Maybe later."

When he brought me my change, I asked him if he knew her last name.

"Embers," he said. "Cathy Embers."

"She talks to you apparently."

"Not much. But everyone talks to the bartender, Kurt."

I munched on peanuts and took my time with my drink. I noticed that Catherine ate none of the peanuts from the bowl by her but downed her cocktail in one gulp. My stool was at the opposite end of the bar, near the door, where the counter curved toward a wall, so I had a diagonal view of her and could finally take a look at her face. Eight lost souls were sitting on their stools between us, but I could see her plainly enough.

I saw neither scars nor any disfigurement. She'd removed her gloves and put them on the bar, but she was keeping her cloak on. *She's not staying long*, I thought — I'd have to be ready to follow her out without seeming to be on her heels. My coat and gloves lay on the stool next to mine and I was trying not to stare at Catherine. Above the bar the TV was on with the sound off so I used that to disguise my scrutiny, watching the Knicks flounder around while darting looks over at her.

Solemnity was in her face, a face with high inelegant cheekbones. I couldn't tell the color of her eyes, but they were not happy. They were large circles in the craters between her brow and cheeks and they would gaze at the whiskey glass, then go to the liquor stock behind the bar, then back to her drink. Nowhere else. And nobody spoke to her, nobody offered to buy her a drink, none of these men acted like men do when a woman enters a bar alone. And not just a woman: an arresting one. Because if she wasn't an exemplary beauty with chiseled symmetrical features, if she wasn't a woman emanating sweetness or vulnerability, she had the allure of someone masking turbulent depths. Or was that just me? My mania for long red hair, dark red hair. Charlotte had that hair, too. Hell, was I seeing what I wanted to see in that mouth expressive even in stillness? Light my fuse, Catherine's mouth said, fan the sparks, and I might explode. She was drinking with an expression the Romans called gravitas, and I was not put off by it. It went with the image I already had of her — a tenacious mourner who'd go to Siberia if June Hazzard's tomb was transferred there.

But everyone else in the bar...they must have known her and knew to keep away. And as Tony had said, she never sat with anyone or accepted free drinks.

The Knicks were losing the game and Hendrix's "The Wind Cries Mary" succeeded Faith Hill on the jukebox. *Good choice*, I wanted to say. *Whoever picked that.* I nursed my rum and Coke at the same clip that Catherine drank her second round, and Tony tended to the other patrons, a sullen bunch talking little, watching the TV, chomping on peanuts.

When Catherine had finished her drink, she pushed up her cloak sleeve and checked her watch. Her face was as grim as I'd yet seen it.

"Thanks, Tony," I said. "Think I'll be going."

"Already? Just one?"

"For tonight. See ya soon."

"Drive safe."

I only had to wait in my car two minutes before Catherine came outside, gliding past me in the parking lot. She was looking straight ahead and didn't seem to notice me, and soon as her Nissan turned into the road, I got moving also.

She led me along for miles, through more of that country darkness. She was driving fast and the roads were slippery. I didn't put on music so I could concentrate fully on the wheel and from my discreet distance I kept watch on her taillights, the yellow ovals, swearing at her because of our speed.

Woman crashes, I thought, *and is rescued by man in car behind her. Love ensues.*

But love or affection or something of the sort was given by her on this night to another. We'd crossed the Hudson, the Rhinebeck Bridge, and what she did was park near the Upstate Films Theater. At its door, fidgeting by the entrance, was a man in a long gray coat and I saw him kiss her on the lips. They met, he dipped his narrow head, he put his hand on her arm, they touched lips, he raised his head. They were outside the theater, which looked like a converted old house, a place showcasing foreign films and independents, un-Hollywood fare, an invaluable theater up here in the "sticks", and there this guy who was tall and willowy, with a straight-edged thatch of dirty-blonde hair, put his mouth on hers. I saw this from a ways off, sitting in my car in the parking lot, but I could see that he had a young face. He looked to be about twenty-five, maybe ten years younger than Catherine Embers.

Side by side, they went through the glass doors to the ticket booth.

The place was presenting *The Skin That I Live In*, Almodovar's psychological thriller. It's a favorite of mine, to tell the truth, a stylish film about revenge, but I wasn't about to sit through it then, *not with them nearby*. Goddamn, I'd be there in my seat, eyes on the screen, trying to take in the story, and all I'd have on my mind would be those two close together in their seats. Maybe he'd be there in the dark, this fucking guy, whoever he was, running his hand through her hair. Letting that red hair play through his fingers, teasing the luscious strands. Just to think of all this pissed me off mightily, and I'd been planning to enjoy my night. So I cut out, drove away, raced back over the Rhinebeck Bridge, and I found a cheap bar in downtown Kingston.

It was a miracle, really, that I drank with restraint and was able to drive myself home later.

SIX

A warm spell began during my time away from the book. Temperatures rose and the sky stayed clear and a bright sun melted the snow. More of it disappeared each day and the ground everywhere was soggy. The fields around the graveyard became marshy, the earth in the woods cold slush. But I didn't stop taking my walks; I slathered oil on my hiking boots and got my exercise every evening. Sometimes I trekked down the main road but I usually marched over the fields and into the woods. My feet would get wet but I didn't mind, and I'd walk where my fancy directed, up leafy hills, through claw-like thickets, along the bank of a stream. I'd listen to the stream rushing by, to the raucous crows sitting on the branches above my head. Nature's noises I never tired of — they were background music for my thoughts — and I didn't miss the sound of my mother's quibbling over commas and semi-colons.

In three or four days, all the snow that had accumulated, the drifts and lumps, was gone.

My rest period over, my mother picked up her story. She still had me doing the chapter about her first boyfriend. This was tricky, because we'd come to her first sexual experience. Both in her notes and in her dictation, my mother was explicit recounting these events, and I felt uncomfortable listening to her, let alone working over these passages, writing and re-writing for her perusal.

She wanted delineated just right the time she first had sex. It happened one summer vacation, on an island in the middle of a lake. I tried to capture what she asked for, portraying her as she described herself: supple-bodied, small-breasted, her black hair abundant. A photo she gave me showed her young face, complete then with a pointed nose and the eagle-sharp eyes. She had the smile of a light-spirited girl, uncalculating (yet watchful — you could see that in the eyes) and she already had her long slender neck. The picture backed up what she'd told me about herself, that she'd had a happy childhood growing up first in Morocco then in New York, that her painter father and photographer mother had been kind and loving. It made me wonder just when the hardening had come into her features. And had that hardening been a natural product of aging only or the manifestation of the twenty eight years of marriage to my father?

More the second reason, I thought, as I examined that photo, and I used the photograph as I wrote the scene where she gave herself to her first boyfriend. I followed her guidance again in describing him — a lanky boy of seventeen who played the violin and studied at Juillard. He told jokes that made her laugh and had a whiskerless baby-boy face. They lived on the same block in Greenwich Village and his parents and hers were friends. That summer they all vacationed together at a bungalow resort in the Catskill Mountains, and during the course of those two months she and Owen became inseparable. It was one August afternoon that the pair of them had gone for a walk to a nearby lake, then rowing on the lake, then over to the lake's island. Anyone could take the boats kept there at the lake's wooden dock, but on this day everybody else was inside. A heat as in an equatorial forest had descended on the Catskills and the whole world but them seemed to be sleeping.

They'd kissed and messed around that summer, but she hadn't gone to the island with him so they could do what they did. The day had begun as a picnic outing, that's about it, and they were lying on a yellow sheet, with sandwiches and cookies in a basket beside them, and lemonade to drink, when the petting and necking became something else.

She didn't resist.

"I was nervous but I wanted him," my mother told me. "You've got to convey that my body was hot for him."

I tried to get that across. But no one I know makes a conscious effort to imagine his mother having sex, whether with his father or a lover or during her youthful years. So for me to sit and write this was grueling, and I found it discomfiting to talk to her about fluff like news or the weather.

At dinner, for example:

"You should get out, mom. It's warm enough now for even you to take a walk."

"I'm fine inside."

"You never go out."

"I go to the store."

"Driving, yeah. I mean out, in the open air."

"When it gets warmer. In the spring."

"Why'd you move upstate at all? Isn't that kinda a weirdo choice?"

"I like the scenery up here."

It could be talk that inane yet I'd know that tomorrow I'd be in the study thinking of her as a girl of fifteen, ballerina thin, her blue summer dress up above her waist. I'd see her with her underpants off, legs around Owen as they heaved and sweat in the grass.

Ouch! My face would turn red when I handed her the pages I'd written. But for all my discomfort, she showed none. She was treating me as if I was a robot, a drudge devoid of sexual feeling, and I didn't like it.

I almost broke out one afternoon and told her about Catherine Embers. Almost, but then I decided against it. Catherine, I felt, had to remain my secret. To tell my mother anything about her was asking for ridicule and disparagement, a hissy fit. She'd go off because any interest I expressed in a woman, emotional interest, interest stronger than the met-her-in-bar-and-screwed-her variety, could represent a threat to the attention I should be lavishing on her book.

"You've become a stalker," she would say (I could hear it). "No girlfriends anymore. You're not up to that. After Charlotte...Am I right? So you stalk? How hopeless can you get?"

Fuuuuuuuck you.

But in the core of my heart, I owned up: I *was* a stalker. I'd mutated into one. By following Catherine after her graveyard visits, driving behind her wherever she went, sometimes in my car and sometimes in my mother's, I'd come to learn where she shopped for food, bought her liquor, purchased goodies for her cat. I watched her and that guy with the youthful face eat out together in Kingston. She lived in a one-floor shingled house ten miles north of Kingston and he

Graveyard Love

lived in the city itself, in a condo community, and they met every weekend and once or twice during the week.

So, yes, I stalked Catherine Embers. And I did feel like I'd gone beyond spying, beyond my stakeouts in the graveyard. Tracking her movements violated decency to an appalling extent. But I did my stalking invisibly. I never menaced her, sent her letters, dialed her number and hung up the phone, or called to utter obscenities. I'd set off from the house at night, after my bath and something to eat, and return home wondering about her. Catherine and that guy. How long had they been going together and how into each other were they?

Their kisses were lip to lip but dry. When they'd meet at a restaurant or outside a movie or when they separated at the end of a night, he'd incline his head and she'd raise her chin and he'd put his hands on her shoulders. They'd smile with locked eyes then and in that posture execute a peck like two birds sharing feed. Not a kiss to inspire envy, not the clinch of people in heat. But with couples you never know; a man and woman reserved in public might do acrobatics in the bedroom. And sometimes after a film and a meal or time at a bar (I'd sit as far from them on the stools as I could), I had seen them drive to his house together and they would both go inside. When that happened, I'd head over to the Fieldhouse Tavern for a nightcap, so I couldn't be positive they spent whole nights together. But it was a safe assumption to think they did. They had a bond that included fucking and maybe they were even two people in love. The sting was painful but I had to take it: Catherine Embers might love this man.

He was a dentist named Ralph Soames. He had his practice there in Kingston. His home phone was accessible through information and I rang him up one night from a disposable cell. Pretending to be someone from a cable company doing a survey on TV viewers, I learned that he was thirty six, once divorced, and without children. His age surprised me, since I'd been thinking he was in his twenties. He had that clean-cut, unlined face, the dirty-blonde hair styled like a frat boy's, a wiry build on his tall frame. I observed him in the evenings leaving his office in a red and blue sweat shirt, carrying a tennis bag, so how he kept himself trim was no mystery. Perhaps Catherine felt a physical tug for him, nothing deeper than that. He seemed ordinary. He got up every morning and went to work, played tennis, liked eating out and going to movies, wore clothes with designer labels on them. What did she see in this bland package? Without knowing something of his mind I couldn't say. But I did want to know whether he himself knew about her graveyard ritual. You're dating someone, sleeping with them, and one day they tell you that every week, two or three times a week, they visit a woman's grave. She died last year at the age of forty-one. *That's sad, you say, but who was she? June Hazzard? What was she to you?* And if he were to hear the noises I'd heard, those libidinous sighs she made in the tomb…Would that be something that scared him away?

I knew I possessed nothing of my father's touch with women. Anyone who beds as many as he did has to be an adept seducer. But I couldn't call upon such prowess and I felt my limitations keenly. What I had to do was the normal thing — go up to Catherine and initiate contact. In all this time, I hadn't even managed that. I didn't have to thrust myself at her, declare I'd become infatuated with her. *I've been watching you. I sit in my window by a telescope and wait for you to arrive at the graveyard. I've stood nearby and listened to you when you're in that vault's back room.* No, candor would fail. I'd sound frightening. *Catherine, your red hair... Could you stand in front of me? With your head at an angle? To the left, down...Push out your hip...Yes...Yes...Yes...*No, clearly I couldn't proceed like a sicko stalker. She'd take flight. But I could do something in the Fieldhouse Tavern. Going up to her there would be within bounds. I could break precedent in the bar and be the one guy to sit beside her, offer to buy her a drink. Or would that be too unoriginal, sure to draw a rebuff? Then I might try something more oddball, but not as extreme as my stalker's pitch. Talk to her, yes, but not like your typical bar guy. *Hello. Can I sit here? If I may...Not to be forward, but...I've noticed you...You visit the graveyard up the road...The one nearby...I myself have a love for graveyards...A real thing for them...Such interesting places... There's an old crumbly one in Baltimore where Poe is buried... And in Cairo, did you know, there's a cemetery where half a million people live...I kid you not...It's gigantic...All these people live between the grave plots and the Egyptians call it The City of the Dead...*Hearing lines like that, grotesque, pompous, she'd either recoil or talk with me. Or maybe she'd just burst out laughing.

My opening came one drizzly night when I saw her at the tavern. She was on her stool near the end of the bar, drinking a screwdriver, wearing black slacks and a black and white sweater. Her cloak was under her on the stool, her car keys on the bar. It was twenty after ten and I'd driven over from the house to have some beers and watch the Knicks play the Spurs. I had never seen her here at this hour and I thought that she must've paid a late night visit to her beloved June Hazzard.

"Tony, a Corona. And gimme a tequila shot with it."

The jukebox was off so the game announcer's voice filled the room. Talk among the patrons was sparse. I looked down the row of torpid men then back at Catherine's care-ravaged face. Alone with her cocktail, eyes opaque, she shed her aura of remoteness as if in that bar there were two distinct zones, hers and everybody else's. *No trespassing*, her expression said, *don't crowd me*. And though I'd formulated what I wanted to say to her, I sat as if nailed to my spot. I moved only my arm to lift my mug, my lips to drink. By the game's end (and the Knicks lost) I'd drunk four beers and done six shots, but some internal check kept me seated. I couldn't bring myself to cross the divide and make the attempt at communication. I didn't address myself to her that night and I watched her exit on unsteady legs, hoping she wouldn't crash in the road.

Something's got to give, I was telling myself, and kept on thinking when I went home to bed. I despised my own hesitancy but felt I'd be able to act on my feelings under different circumstances. If only Catherine had no boyfriend and I no mother whom I lived with. *Those two block everything*, I thought, but on further reflection, I pinned it down. Even more than this Ralph Soames guy, it was my mother, my living arrangement, that was holding me back. With a woman I cared nothing for, just met in a bar, I could talk. I could loosen up and let libido guide me. When the prime goal for the night was fucking, I'd lay myself out there. I'd say to the woman I was talking to we'd have to do our fucking in her bed because I lived at home with my mother and it would be dicey to take her there. Some women ran from me when I said this, some unleashed derision — "How old are you? Still living with your mother? Does she still wash your underwear?" (Answers: thirty-five, yes, no) — but most were too bombed to reverse course. "My place then," is what I'd hear. "Finish your drink." In that arena of pickled brains and lonely bodies I felt no stigma revealing how I lived, and if one woman sniggered after I said I resided at home, I'd move down the bar counter to another. I'd persist with an insouciance I couldn't dig up when faced with the prospect of accosting Catherine.

So, the stalking. The watching. The tagging after her at night when she ate out with Soames or trolled the aisles of the mini mart. But even I felt debased doing this, and with what I knew of stalking, with what I'd seen of its consequences, I realized that I had to stop. I was playing with mental fire. Once you begin the stalking game, fall into the stalking vortex, there's no telling where things will end. And I was at the lip of the whirlpool. I'd begun to fantasize about breaking into Soames' house at night, on an evening when they were out together, hiding myself in his bedroom closet. When they came home, I'd confirm for myself whether they were fucking. But if I did that, how much further would I be willing to go? And who was to say that looking at them would be a turn-on? Seeing her under Ralph Soames, or straddling him, might make me violently angry at the guy. The stalking syndrome, I told myself, is a no-win proposition, and as if I needed convincing on this, I called to mind what had happened with my father.

It concerned a woman client he had. This person, Jill Devers, had come onto him during the time he was defending her but amazingly enough he said nix, keeping his cock in his pants to maintain professional conduct. Jill Devers kept writing and phoning him, though, her overtures becoming insults. This was after he got her acquitted of a cocaine buying charge. Go figure. You can read about the episode in toto in my *New Yorker* piece (the October 27th, 2003 issue), but the long and the short of it all was she killed him. Unlike me, she was a stalker who hounded her target, who dispatched warnings. She mailed him souvenirs like her underpants and left him messages telling him what he'd done that week, where he'd been, that she'd been watching him. Who was that woman he went to dinner with? she'd ask. Did he love her or was she just a fuck? She sent him boxes containing homemade dolls carved from wax, each doll with a photo of his face on the head. One effigy might have pins stuck through its eyes, another, the next week, darts protruding from its chest. "I won't be ignored," was her underlying message, but my father did ignore her. He and my mother had separated, and my mother had instructed her lawyers to draw up divorce papers. My father had moved out of our Brooklyn brownstone to a hotel on Central Park South, the Essex House. From there, living in style, he went on with his professional life and his carnal escapades, and maybe it was a liking for mischief that drove him to keep Jill Devers at bay. He'd told me about her harassment; I beseeched him to sick the cops on her ass. "Get a protective order against her," I said. He laughed. The dictates of machismo and his self-conceit made him underestimate Jill Devers. And it must've stoked his vanity to know that she was tortured over him, that this young woman (she was twenty-seven) had fixated on him erotically. At lunch with me one time he dismissed her as benign, waved a smug contemptuous hand. But Jill Devers wasn't so benign. She breezed into the Essex House one night and strode past the front desk. She boarded an elevator. It would come to light that she'd phoned that day, asking for my father's room number. Execution style she did it, two point blank to his head, and nobody said they heard the shots.

Room service found him in the morning.

Anyway, getting back to stalking, what I was saying before: the Jill Devers episode is evidence of what stalking and obsession can do to the mind. Namely, warp it. Lead it down into the maelstrom of homicidal rage. *Catherine Embers, Ralph Soames — why do you have to be together? You, Soames, you merit her affection? Go fuck yourself. You don't even know her. I know her. I alone know that she loves a dead woman and visits her grave as frequently as she goes out with you. So scram!*

See what I'm driving at. You lay in bed at night with thoughts like these and it's not long before you imagine erasing Ralph Soames. Not Catherine. I'd never harm her. But Soames, the obstruction — you picture yourself buying a handgun, ringing his condo door at night, forcing him in when he answers the door, lying him down on his back in bed and jamming a pillow over his face. Then boom, you fire into the pillow. Silent death. Obstruction gone. Simple as pie...

By the way, to backtrack again momentarily, they caught Jill Devers on my tip. When I went to the station, I told the police that criminal lawyer though he was, my father had no known enemies. "Does that include your mother?" they asked me, and considering the state of my parents' marriage, I couldn't say she wasn't hostile towards him. They must've pegged her as a suspect. But I did mention the Devers woman and her hang-up with my father, and that led the cops in her direction.

No surprise; it's a theory of mine that most stalkers do get themselves arrested. I haven't done a scientific study of the question, but I bet I'm right. Stalkers are too controlled by their obsessions to keep a low profile. They end up doing something outlandish, whether it be murder or rape or a theft of an object from the person they're obsessed with. And compulsion leads to carelessness, mistakes while doing the crime. Many of them don't want to remain incognito, mere spies or peeping toms. They have to make a statement about their fevered love and the crime is their formal declaration of that love, their bid for attention.

You see, Catherine. You think I don't mean it? I killed Ralph Soames because I love you. That's it. I haven't lost my mind. I wouldn't shoot a man for no good reason. It's not psychosis talking, it's love.

That was the thinking I could see coming on and I told myself to stop obsessing before I suffered a breakdown. From fantasy to action, how far a distance was it? With that gun I imagined buying I could do my mother after eradicating Soames. By deleting her, I could unburden myself of her book. My pride wouldn't let me abandon the book, but her death would. And what liberation I would feel not having to hash over everything in her life, her sexual initiation as a teenager...

Something has to give, I'd been telling myself; I have to release the pressure inside. And who can say what I might have done had everything not drastically changed. To my consternation, I discovered that somebody else was following Catherine Embers. Another person was spying on her, another man. *For fuck's sake*, I thought. *He's encroaching on my territory*. But then I felt my outrage peter out and saw how entertaining this all had become.

The other man tailing her was Ralph Soames.

SEVEN

I noticed him one evening when she came to the graveyard. Her white Nissan was by the cemetery gate and she was in her black cloak walking past the tombs and headstones toward June Hazzard's vault. Nothing off-kilter in any of this and I at my telescope in my room panned up as if with a camera to look at the pinewoods beyond her. The sun had set behind those trees, providing them with a backdrop of sky brilliant as molten copper. I let out a whistle. I valued the view I had, a view that anytime could bring something splendid. Vibrant color. An abstract expressionist cloud design done in fiery tints. If I was in my room and saw Catherine's car pulling up, I'd look through my telescope and over at her less for her in and out of herself than for Catherine as a sliver of the landscape. There'd she be in that cloak, with her long red hair, under a sky forbiddingly gray or burnt orange like tonight's. Sometimes I'd put on my coat and boots and dash over to the vault to listen to Catherine moan in the back, but for the most part nowadays I was keeping clear of the graveyard. I knew Catherine's ritual backwards and forwards and had learned all I could from pure observation.

Then Soames, that evening, shook everything up. I'd risen from the telescope and was turning away from my bedroom window when I saw his car coming up the road — a silver Jaguar. Transfixed, I put my face to the pane. I'd followed him and Catherine often enough to know his vehicle instantly. He whizzed on past the graveyard entrance and past his girlfriend's parked car, but he hadn't gone far past the house when he braked to a stop dead smack in the road.

I sat down by my telescope again, the lens my eyes. The Jaguar was there to my left and I watched Ralph Soames in a blue overcoat open his door and step out of the car. He was peering back toward the cemetery. His squarish face looked aggrieved. I went out on a limb and made the deduction that standing here at night in his bulky coat, with a ski cap on his head, was not his idea of a pleasurable time. He seemed to be staring at Catherine's car, perhaps wondering where she'd gone. She was nowhere in sight and he hadn't seen her go into June Hazzard's vault.

For about five minutes he stood in the road, not even budging when a car approached. The driver had to swerve, honking, to avoid him. Then he got back into his Jaguar and did a one-eighty, and he drove off the way he'd come. He moved from left to right in my lens. I don't know whether he stopped down the road to wait for Catherine to drive on by him, but if he did he had a long wait. After finishing up in the vault, Catherine drove off in the other direction. She was heading no doubt to her post-graveyard haunt, the Fieldhouse Tavern.

So that was that night, something unprecedented. And as I said, my initial reaction was anger at Soames. He had no business interloping here, showing up in our domain. *I* shared the cemetery region with Catherine. Not him. Me. It ticked me off that he was spying on her, sneaking around behind her back.

I can spy on Catherine, I thought. *I've taken that prerogative. But Catherine's unaware of my existence and what she doesn't know can't hurt her. I'm not her boyfriend. I haven't betrayed any trust she put in me.*

Only when I calmed down did I grasp the implications of his private eye act. Catherine and Ralph were having problems and suspicion had reared its vile head. Maybe he'd asked her straightforward questions about where she went three evenings a week and she had given him cryptic answers.

He thinks there's somebody else, I thought. *That she's seeing somebody.*

So happens she is — a dead person.

Hard to compete with the dead, huh, Soames? A dead woman, no less?

What do you do? Want me to tell you what to do?

Get in line, mister. Get in line.

EIGHT

For the next three nights, I didn't go out to follow Catherine or Ralph. Wearied from my work on the book, I turned in early each night. Catherine visited the tomb once; Ralph didn't drive up behind her. What went on elsewhere with them, I didn't know. But it seemed like I had two viable options: let their relationship run its course, wherever that led, or do something to hasten the split I saw developing between them.

A no-brainer choice. Fuck them up. I'd tolerated Ralph seeing Catherine long enough, and with the distrust in her he was exhibiting, did I need to do much to widen the rift?

Yet again a disposable cell was my weapon of choice.

"That you, Ralph? You're Ralph Soames?"

"Who is this?"

"Sorry to disturb you on a Sunday evening."

"This is Ralph Soames."

"You watching anything? Think I can hear it."

"Pardon?"

"Home by yourself in front of the TV?"

"I don't recognize your voice."

"You've never heard it," I said. "But my question is, what's Catherine doing tonight?"

No answer bounced back from that and I thought I heard Soames' breathing stop.

"You hear me, Ralph? It's a legitimate question."

"If you want to talk to me, we should meet somewhere."

"You have a deep voice," I said. "Didn't figure you for that."

"Listen, asshole—"

"Don't know why, I never heard a dentist with a deep voice. Always guys with these low monotonous drones. Head back. Open up. That's it. A little more."

"Are you going anywhere with this?"

"I can say open up, too. Don't have to be a dentist to say that."

"So?"

"And she does — Catherine — open up. She opens up for me."

I heard a beep and nothing after. On his phone, he'd hit the OFF button.

Same night, an hour later, I called him again. He didn't say hello when he picked up and I could hear an announcer's voice talking about a "double major."

Hockey.

"Ever take Catherine to a game, Ralph? Does she like sports?"

"You mean you don't know?"

"I don't dwell on sports when I'm with her."

"Not you. Why would you?"

"There's other stuff we concern ourselves with."

"So you said. She opens up for you, spreads her legs..."

"That's right."

"How lucky you are. You're a fortunate man."

He didn't sound surprised we were talking again and I thought I might've waited too long to call him back. During the hour, he'd composed himself. But he also sounded a tad derisive, as if he'd already sussed me out and knew I couldn't be seeing Catherine. Had she told him about June Hazzard? Her visits to the tomb? I'd felt she'd keep that information from him, but maybe she'd talked. Maybe after the night he'd followed her to the graveyard, he'd peppered her with questions and she'd shared, divulging the identity of the "other person." He might know what she was doing inside the vault, while I still didn't. The fucker. And whatever he knew, it didn't repel him? He carried on with their relationship?

Indulgent guy. Your girlfriend's got a thing for a dead woman, you find out, and you're cool with it.

"Don't know why you say I'm lucky," I said.

"It's the only way to describe your success."

"I make my own luck."

"Now I know you're not serious."

"For a guy who's girlfriend's playing around on him—"

"If she is, it isn't with you."

"If?"

"Or I should amend that. If it's with you, she hasn't given you squat."

"You don't even know me."

"A hand job at best. If you're truly *lucky*, you got that much from her."

"I—"

"And now that you mention it, I think I may know you."

"Yeah. You know I'm the other guy she's seeing."

"No, but I'm not oblivious."

The beep, the dead line, and I felt throbbing in my neck. The call hadn't gone one bit as I'd expected.

Around seven the next evening, the doorbell rang. My hand clutched and I almost dropped my cooking pan. We never had visitors and I couldn't remember the last time the bell had rung.

I put the pan down on the stove, turned the flame low under it. I'd smeared it with olive oil and salted the chicken breast on the counter beside me.

"Who is that? Did the doorbell ring?"

My mother down in the basement, working on a new pottery masterpiece.

"It did," I said. "Don't know."

"Can you find out?"

"I intend to, ma."

I opened the door to find Ralph Soames, ruddy in the cold, blonde hair neat. He had his blue overcoat on but no scarf and no gloves.

"Can I help you with something?"

He didn't waste words. "Was it you?"

"Excuse me."

"The *other* guy."

"If you're looking for someone..."

"It's you," he said. "I can hear it. Same voice."

I might've slammed the door on him if my mother hadn't come in then, clomping through the cellar doorway behind me.

"Kurt, who is that?"

"No one, ma."

"I can see it's somebody."

Soames crooked his neck to peek over my shoulder and his eyebrows curled like question marks when he saw my mother: a white-haired, bird-faced woman in black tights and a long black sweater, her hands gooey with clay.

"Pathetic," he said, smiling. "Fucking figures."

"Do you know this man?" my mother asked, still somewhere behind me.

"A guy who lives with his mother."

"This is nobody, ma."

"Your son's a peach. He calls other men to talk about their girlfriends."

I turned to my mother and rolled my eyes, scoffing at the encounter, but she had her bird-eyes glued to Soames as if trying to see into his head.

"Obscene calls," Soames continued. "Know what I mean?"

I looked at him again. "You should get off this stoop. And get your goddamn car off this driveway."

"You call again," he said, "and I'll call the cops."

"I'll call them myself if you don't get off our property."

He shook his head and I shut the door waiting to hear his car start.

"Our property?" my mother said. "Since when is this house our property?"

"Since I moved in? I don't know. Since I took over on the book?"

"Don't get any ideas."

"Only saying."

"What *are* you saying?"

"Who's writing it now and who couldn't write it by herself before?"

"I have clay to heat, Kurt. Don't involve me with your girl stuff please."

"I didn't tell the guy to come here."

"You did something to upset him. That's obvious."

"And I didn't ask you to come upstairs."

"I don't care what you do on your own time, Kurt. Just keep it away from the house."

"You believe what he said? That was total bullshit."

My mother sniffed the air. "Is something in the kitchen burning?"

The olive oil — I could hear it sizzling.

Fuck.

"I forgot—"

"You better get it," she said.

I ran back to the frying pan, waving an arm against the smoke, and my mother returned to the basement.

Soames, I saw, remained on our property. He was sitting in his car in the driveway, behind mine. The ceiling light in the Jaguar lit him. He had both arms on the steering wheel and his chin on his forearms. That vanilla-bland face — it was looking straight ahead at no discernible section of the house. Was he challenging me, the son of a bitch, trying to lure me outside and into a physical confrontation? I watched him through the kitchen window, my finger holding the drape back an inch, and I had to give the guy props. No retiring dentist, he. To sit there in our driveway, saying *fuck you* by doing it, showed balls.

Coatless, I opened the front door and stepped out. Frigid air assaulted my face. But I kept on going, across the road, straight toward the Jaguar, and Soames raised his middle finger at me through the driver's side window. I thought I could see a smirk on his face.

"You want your ass kicked? I'll take your fuckin' head off with a baseball bat."

Soames took the hint and backed up. The light inside the car went out. I stopped in the driveway and watched him go, and he gave his horn a prolonged honk as he sped away.

"Moron!" I said.

So no catharsis, just name-calling, and I didn't understand how Soames had found me. Based on what he knew of me, what would he tell Catherine? She didn't know I existed and the picture he'd paint of me would suck. I'd be tarnished in her eyes before I got the chance to introduce myself. What was I saying? I'd had countless chances to introduce myself and because of fear had never done it. Idiotic, but fact was fact. The more I thought about it, standing in my yard, the more imperative it seemed that he not get the chance to tell her about me. I couldn't allow that. I had to get to him before he spoke to her. Catch up with him, talk to him. Apologize if need be. I'd have to find a way to persuade him to keep our phone chats between ourselves.

Car keys, coat, gloves, and the aluminum baseball bat dug from my closet — I collected what I needed to venture out after him. I didn't run the engine to let it warm up but put the car on the road right away. I had two alternatives: drive toward Catherine's house in case Soames was going there or drive toward his. At an intersection farther along, depending on which house I'd visit, I'd have to turn left or right. But what if he'd phoned her already? Or texted. Then I'd be fucked. His description of me to her would be done.

While I contemplated this, enraged with myself for having called Soames, Catherine's car went by. Her Nissan passed in the opposite direction. *Graveyard visiting time*, I thought, and then: *good*. With her over there, I'd drive to Soames'. But what if she wasn't heading to the graveyard? Her intended destination might be my house. Soames might have telephoned her and she now planned to see me, the creep, for herself. This meant she'd ring the bell and my mother would answer. Catherine and my mother in conversation, discussing me, a nightmare scenario. I couldn't do nothing and let that happen. Of all the goddamn things I didn't want to happen...

Shit. How I had let everything fall apart, and so fast?

I braked, U-turned, pressed on the gas. Drove back through the dark praying I'd get there before they started talking. I'd feel awkward standing between them if they spoke, but I needed at least to be there to have an influence over the meeting.

Her car was parked at the cemetery gate. I didn't see Catherine in the driveway or standing on our stoop. No sign of her in the graveyard. She'd probably gone into the graveyard and entered the tomb already, but I didn't want to go over there to look. I'd use up time doing that and she might have rung the bell and been let inside by my mother. They could be talking away, Catherine pumping my mother for information about me, my mother wondering what in the hell was going on, two aggressive visitors in one night.

I pulled back into the driveway, shut the ignition off. Now through the front door and inside again, panting. But I met nothing and no one, no drama whatsoever. The living room and kitchen were empty and I could hear my mother tapping at something in the basement.

The house's serenity seemed to mock me.

Hysterical jerk.

To re-collect myself, I got back into my car. I adjusted the mirrors so I could see the graveyard, the gate especially. I let the motor idle and the heat blast. Unpleasant but true: I kept coming up against an incontrovertible fact. My approach to Catherine, however I did it, would be dicey. It would have to be. Nothing I could think of to say would sound acceptable. I love you? I've been watching you? I've been known to get aroused thinking of you? It all sounded slimy, like words she would run from. I saw no getting around that. But I knew I had to do it here, tonight, after she and June finished communing, and if Ralph had filled her in about my phone calls, so be it. Zero hour was at hand.

Catherine still hadn't left the tomb when the Jaguar reappeared. Soames slid off the road and stopped on the shoulder behind her Nissan and sprang out his door running. The cocksucker sprinted straight through the gate and into the cemetery and I don't think I lost a second getting outside also. Eager to catch him, I slipped, and the fall saved me. I hit my knee on the frozen ground and that slowed me up. Restored me to intelligent thought. Did Soames know where he was going and mean to invade June Hazzard's vault. Though I'd never interrupted Catherine there, maybe he would. And if he went in, I had a hunch she wouldn't like it. They were having problems, I shouldn't forget that, and I should let him dig his own hole.

I walked across the road, veered left, and positioned myself by a gap in the fence. Soames wasn't far from June Hazzard's vault but he was looking all around the cemetery, a broad-shouldered shape in the coppery moonlight.

"Catherine."

I saw him say her name but in a whisper. She couldn't have heard him. And when he took out his sleek iPhone and speed-dialed a number, it became clear he didn't want her to hear him. A music tone trilled in June Hazzard's vault and Soames touched a button on his phone to cut it off.

Up in the dark a blackbird squawked. The cold was biting into my ears and leaves were scudding across the ground, over my feet. From just outside the tomb, Soames stood looking into it, his fisted hands on his hips, shoulders going up and down in his padded jacket, and then he advanced into the tomb, engulfed by its darkness.

The crow in the sky cried again. But that was nothing, a far-off squeak, compared to the scream that came from the vault. It had come from Catherine and no horror movie scream could have sounded more chilling. I thought she was being attacked. I lifted my leg to step through the hole in the fence, but her scream was followed by the sound of her yelling, cursing in a furious voice at Soames.

"You motherfucker! Fucking asshole. Who told you you could follow me here?"

I hesitated, one leg through the fence, nose in between the bars.

"Catherine..."

"Get the fuck out."

"This is sick."

"Get out! "

"I'd like an explanation."

"An explanation?" Catherine laughed, gave a guttural cackle, and I heard disdain ring out from her voice. "You demand an explanation. Mister Ralph Soames."

"I do."

"Fuck off. Now you know me. You can leave."

"No. Not until..."

Soames' voice trailed off and I couldn't hear what he said next. Just Catherine shouting again, telling him to go.

"I won't!" he said. "I will not."

"You fucking loser."

A grunting noise reached me from inside the tomb and nothing came afterwards but silence. I waited for Catherine or Soames to talk, but neither of them did. The silence hung there. Then Catherine emerged, her head held high, red hair aflutter in the wind. She sashayed along in her black cloak and her black leather boots, but I stayed over near the vault. Where was Soames? Wouldn't he chase her? Catherine's car rumbled to life and I began to feel uneasy, touched with foreboding. I stepped through the hole and ran to the vault. Inside was darkness — no candles burning. I took my flashlight from my jacket but before I could switch it on, I tripped over something in the front chamber. Something soft was on the floor.

"Goddamn."

I'd regained my footing, one hand against the tomb wall for balance. My beam of light illuminated Soames down there at my feet: his gaping mouth, his open vacant eyes, the blood pooling at the back of his head. Blood lay splashed on the black stone slab where an unlit candle stood, and when I got down on my knees and put my head to his chest, I heard nothing. No heartbeat. I felt nauseous being close to that blood, but I kept my head there till I'd counted to sixty.

"Goddamn," I said again, alone in the darkness of the vault.

Ralph Soames was dead.

NINE

So now the tomb, built for one, contained two. And Catherine had fled. I did also after listening for a pulse, and I drove over to her house that night to see if she had gone back there. She had; the Nissan was in her driveway. Whether she had willfully murdered Ralph Soames with a blow or he had died inadvertently — pushed perhaps, his skull splitting open on the black slab — she did not seem to be panicking. She had not struck out for the interstate highway. As I took my car past the shingled house, driving slowly down the residential street, I could see lights on within and I could only speculate on what she was doing inside. Drinking? Packing luggage? Watching TV as if nothing had happened? From my perspective, something sure as hell had happened, and its gravity kept me up all night, my head aching. I paced in the candlelit dark of my room, lay down, got up, sat in my blue chair, drank a pot of green tea. I was so unsettled by this turn of events I couldn't take in food or keep down alcohol. I'd tried both that evening, and vomited. I couldn't watch a movie either; the images blurred before my eyes. Sober thinking was the most I could do, and through the wee hours of the morning I did that, playing Bela Bartok's string quartets (I have them all on CD) for company.

On the surface, Ralph Soames' death was a favorable development. My fantasies of his demise had come true and I hadn't needed to commit a crime, endanger myself. If I went up to Catherine now, I'd know she was a woman alone. No man was in her life. But she was also, possibly, a murderer. Or at a minimum, someone with a dead body on her hands, lying there in that tomb. She hadn't fetched the police that night which led me to believe she'd hit him with homicidal intent, but what would she do to hide the body? She couldn't leave it in the vault. Someone, a graveyard attendant, would light upon it eventually. But would that prove anything? A dead man found in a vault would be a mystery, and as far as Catherine knew, there'd been no witnesses to the incident. If police dusted for fingerprints at the scene, they'd find hers (not mine, I thought, since I'd always worn my gloves in there), but she could answer that by admitting her visits, saying June Hazzard had been her friend. There'd be people the cops questioned who'd know she and Soames had been seeing one another, but that wouldn't get her arrested and charged. Nothing would if she kept her composure, didn't slip up, and no prosecutor would bring the case to trial on such meager evidence. So she was free and clear, it seemed to me, regardless of what had occurred in the tomb, but to stay untouched she'd have to keep away from the tomb until the body was discovered. No sweat: she wouldn't dare cling to habit with a body in there with her. Come and go as if the body wasn't there? She wouldn't do that. Not even she, I thought, would do that. She'd either stop her visits till she got word of the body's discovery or rid the tomb of the body herself.

Graveyard Love

The sixth Bartok quartet had concluded, allowing silence into my room, when I jumped from my chair and swore at myself. How feeble-minded could I get? Catherine was at home, safe for now, and the body was out of sight in the tomb, but Soames' car was by the cemetery gate where everyone would see it come morning. In my tunnel vision, my obsession with Catherine and how Soames' death might benefit me, I'd overlooked this mundane detail. The graveyard attendants would find the silver Jaguar when they arrived for work, and unless they conspired to take it (counting it a blessing to have a Jaguar fall into their laps), the discovery would set off an investigation. Who did the vehicle belong to? Why was it sitting here? They'd notify the cops and the cops would check the license plate and registration. Etcetera, etcetera. In the blink of an eyelash, they'd trace the car to Ralph Soames. As a dentist he undoubtedly had a receptionist, and if not that, somebody somewhere who cared about him, a male friend, a tennis buddy, and that somebody might report him missing. The logical place to search first would be where his car was found, the graveyard, and if the attendants didn't find him in the tomb, the police would when they did their hunt. By tomorrow night, I realized, they might have Catherine on their suspect list.

Again, though, would it matter? Would they have enough to charge her with murder? I'd told myself no but now I warned myself to take nothing for granted. I didn't know what they might find. If Catherine had scratched Soames during their confrontation in the vault and had his skin under her fingernails or if he had nicked her and had her blood on him, the cops would have physical evidence, DNA stuff. Catherine could say she and Soames had been lovers so of course he had her skin cells on her, but to the police their having been lovers would elevate her as a suspect. Whatever. The point was, there were innumerable possibilities I hadn't first taken account of, and as I stood by my window with a pounding heart, I saw that I'd have to act myself, tonight, before it got light out, to clean up Catherine's mess. I couldn't let the car sit there till morning.

The temperature outside was sub-zero. Or it felt that cold with the wind chill factor. Streams of icy air blew across my face as I ran down the driveway and across the road and I could hear the gusts in the woods wailing, rising and falling in pitch. I'd lined myself with thermal underclothes underneath jeans and a layering of shirts and I had my parka collar turned up high. With that and my scarf, my knit cap and gloves, little of my bare skin was exposed but what was open to the merciless wind burned at the touch of its coldfire breath — my lips, my nose, my cheeks. I could feel the searing up inside my nostrils. Ignore it, I said, ignore and carry on, and if I did talk to Catherine one day, I'd tell her what I'd tried to do on this night. I'd explain that I'd risked frostbite for her. Maybe she would feel something for me then.

The car door, driver's side, was unlocked, and the ceiling light came on when I pulled it open. Lowering my head, I saw that the ignition was empty. This didn't surprise me; if anything, I'd been expecting it. No keys here meant the one for the engine probably was in Soames's coat or pants, inside the tomb, and since I didn't know how to hot-wire cars, I'd have to go and dig. Like it or not, I'd have to put my hands on his corpse.

The quarter moon lit my way through the cemetery. The ground was like rock, the grass white with rime. None of the noisy crows were around so the wind from the woods had no sonic competition and it was howling like a living thing, like some sad monster which had lost its mate. With every step I took that wind pummeled me and every breath from my mouth was steam.

The tomb, thankfully, was warmer. Igloo effect, I suppose, no space inside for the air to whirl and bite. I'd entered from the moonlight into darkness and just past the threshold I paused, reaching in my parka for my pocket flash. I didn't want to trip over Soames again.

As I had earlier, I looked at him lying on the tomb's floor. My light shone on his open mouth and glaring eyes. The eyes and his face, that preppie face, registered nothing - no contortion of horror or fear. However he'd been killed, he'd been caught off-guard: one instant he'd been alive, locking horns with Catherine; the next, gone.

I got down on the floor, my chin to the stone, and scrutinized him. He lay face up with a pool of dried blood underneath his head. In the pinpoint of light I could see the spot where his blonde hair was matted and the skin broken, not far above the base of his neck. He and Catherine had been face to face, I assumed, addressing each other, before she struck him. So unless she had the speed of a cat-quick boxer she couldn't have leaped behind him for her blow. That would've been a life-ending slug and she would've had to have a heavy object to boot. The rent in his head hadn't come from bare hands. I looked at the wound and the brownish red bloodstains on one corner of the marble slab, and from these I deduced with near certainty that Catherine had lunged at him during the argument. She'd given him a shove, he'd lost his balance. He'd fallen backwards against the slab, striking an edge and cracking his skull.

I stood up and wiped dust off my jacket. Murder hadn't happened in here, I thought, but something had that was troubling nonetheless. What, legally? A fatal accident, nothing premeditated. In lawyer's terms, manslaughter.

You do jail time for that, too, I thought. *Ten years, twenty, enough time to ruin a life.* The wisest thing would be to move the body along with the Jaguar. Make Ralph Soames disappear forever. That would cover all the bases and help Catherine greatly; the corpse was an item she couldn't handle herself. She might return here with plans to hide the body, but I couldn't see her lifting it up to carry it out of the tomb. She was in shape, my Catherine, I could tell that from her lightfooted walk, the elegance of her straight-backed carriage, but she didn't strike me as a bodybuilding woman. And Soames had size. I put him at about six feet two, in the vicinity of one ninety. Unless she did the gruesome, cut him up in here to cart him away in pieces, she'd never tote his body from the vault. I'd have to do that for her also, if it was to be done at all.

Stooping beside him, I searched for Ralph Soames' car keys. I kept my gloves on as I tried the left waist pocket of his blue overcoat, then the right. Zilch. I went on to his pants, the black Hilfiger's, and I grit my teeth as I forced myself to squeeze my hand into his right hip pocket. From the cold or rigor mortis he felt hard to my touch, his sinewy thigh like petrified wood under the lining of his pants. I shuddered to feel that, my fingers tensing, but then my glove touched a metal nub and I pulled out a ring of keys.

I held them up to my flashlight. Six were on the ring and so was the push-button car alarm activator.

Soames' watch said half past three. In about three hours, before dawn, I had both his body and the car to get rid of. Not to mention the bloodstains in here. But I hadn't brought a shovel for grave digging with me nor any scouring products, and I knew I'd be facing significant risk however I did this clean-up. What I could do was put the body in the car and drive it someplace, though I'd be fucked if a cop pulled me over, if for some fluky reason he told me to open my trunk. And would Ralph Soames, all six feet two of him, even fit in that compartment? The boot was tiny. Laid out straight he'd never go in and now he was lying here stiff. I'd have to bend Soames all over, snap his bones and stubborn dead muscles to have any chance of hiding him there.

You better love me, Catherine, I thought. *Who would do this for you? Go to the extremes I have for you. When I meet you, Catherine, you better...*

The wind was unflagging, the cold in my joints and facial pores. I'd left the insulation of the tomb and was walking with Ralph Soames on my shoulder. Adrenaline must have squirted from my glands because his body felt light. His stiffness helped; he didn't flop around like a piece of loose meat. Yet I wasn't moving toward his car, but toward the woods, across the open field behind the cemetery, and here the unobstructed wind was at its fiercest, blowing against my face and chest as if it was a sentient force loath to let me into the forest.

I got to the pines and dropped Ralph Soames at my feet. I could smell pine needles and ground ice the wind skipped off. Turning, I looked back at the cemetery, and I gasped at its ethereal beauty under the cloud-hazed glow of the moon. The white mausoleums, the crosses, the alabaster tombstones — in this lunar light, this veiled luminescence, were they a mirage? My whole night seemed like an hallucination.

With a knee dip and a rapid straightening, I scooped Soames up and hoisted him over my right shoulder. I held him around the waist to keep him there and used my left hand to take my flashlight out of my jacket again. Then I was pressing ahead through underbrush, beneath the overhanging branches. A dirt path the width of two arm lengths opened out before me and dry leaves and twigs broke under my sneakers. Off to my left was the sound of running water, a gurgle below the wailing wind. That noise came from the stream I knew, the brook that ran on for miles in these woods. Nearly everywhere it was too wide to cross without getting wet but I did enjoy sitting and listening to it. The seat I liked was a toppled oak that a storm had killed sometime past; immense but ailing, the tree had been leveled by winds like tonight's. It lay about half a mile down the stream bank, a stone's throw off the path, and I hoped I could make it that far with Soames — the adrenaline in me was wearing off.

These are my *woods,* I thought, *this is* my *territory.* It seemed as if all my walking here had been a preparation for this night, so I'd know where to go with a body to stash it. Flashlight or no, I would have found the uprooted oak. I knew how far to walk on the path, would have known without the aid of light where to duck under a low-hanging branch and bat aside a cord of thistles. My back and right shoulder hurt from Soames' weight but on the plus side the wind had abated and my heart and blood were producing heat. I scarcely even felt the cold anymore.

As I moved off the path, I carried Ralph Soames through the leafless bushes. My feet struggled with spiky rocks. The burble of the stream was close and I smelled damp moss and wet leaves, a mixture as rich in the nose as compost. Then the water came into view, silvery in the light from the moon, and I stepped out onto the open bank. Again, unfolding my arms, I let Soames drop. He hit the bank with a thump, lying face down in the pebbles and dirt.

I was next to the dead oak tree, exhausted. To gather myself I sat down on the trunk and tried to rub the pain from my shoulder. I'd pocketed my flashlight and was staring at Catherine's ex in the moonlight. His blonde hair had become unkempt and his fair skin looked waxy. Odd, but sitting here with him, having this moment, being closer to him than I'd ever been when he was alive, I almost expected animation out of him, a show of resentment against me.

"You shouldn't have meddled," I imagined him saying. "Let the fruitcake take her punishment."

The wind was a forceful menace again, pitched in the glass-shattering range. I heard branches breaking, the crack of tree bark. The sounds brought me out of my reverie, and I kicked Soames in the leg. His corpse talking? Get real. That was horror film hokum and I banished it from my thoughts.

I got myself low alongside Soames and rolled him slantwise across the bank. Under the oak's trunk, where the ground sloped toward the water, there was an empty space, something like a den, that had formed naturally when the tree had fallen. On my knees by the water I packed him in as far as he would go, leaving him with his face in the dirt, arms along his sides. His body fit with room to spare; someone standing on top of the oak, above him on the trunk, wouldn't be able to see Soames. You'd have to be about where I was for that or in the water going upstream. And in this weather, this far out in the woods, who'd be passing? In all my daily walks out here, I'd come across hikers a dozen times at most, and that had been in the spring or summer. Never in the winter. So to keep him here would do, I thought, would work temporarily, and tomorrow night, when I had time and a shovel, I could come out here and bury him. See to it that his body vanished for good.

TEN

I'd never driven a car as high-end as a Jaguar. The silver racer had tremendous pick-up and bucket seats. It handled so well I could've gunned it down a ski-slalom course, but at this early an hour of the morning, no such skill was necessary. I met no traffic on the back country roads and scattered cars and trucks on the highway. I took the New York State Thruway south, doing a consistent sixty-five, and got to the Tappan Zee Bridge by six. The commute from the suburbs hadn't started yet, and as I was driving over the Hudson, I looked downriver toward New York City. Visibility was limited, the pallid darkness of the dying night fogged with wisps of gray.

The Thruway goes through Yonkers to the Bronx. I stayed on it when it became something else, the Major Deegan, and slowed to a crawl when tie-ups began. The sun had risen, clouds were out; I saw a news station chopper overhead, the eye in the sky above the rush hour snarls. It'd been ages since I'd done city driving with the clamorous horns and the bumper to bumper frustration, and I was happy to see the majestic exterior of Yankee Stadium, all white, coming up on my left. That was my landmark, and I inched through the traffic to the exit ramp.

My plan was uncomplicated. Find a street where parking was legal. Collect all the registration documents and anything that might identify the owner. Leave the keys and abandon the Jaguar, then get the subway and ride on down to Grand Central Station. By nightfall I'd be home, and it stood to reason the car would catch somebody's eye. It might be taken and kept, it might be stripped down for parts.

ELEVEN

I felt sixteen, adolescent again, when I walked into the house that night. Instead of returning home in the morning, I'd opted to nap in the city first, taking a room at the Hotel Carter, the timeworn fleabag on Forty Third Street. It was after eleven and I knew my mother would be waiting up, teed off at me. She'd want to know where I'd been and why I hadn't called and she'd tell me that she'd smoked more cigarettes today than she liked.

The light over the stoop was on and likewise the pink-yellow ceiling bulb in the foyer. No other lights and I didn't hear my mother. I closed the front door as the cab that had brought me from the bus stop in town backed out of our driveway, and went up the two flights of stairs to my room. I didn't look to see whether my mother was in her room on the second floor.

Ready for her questions, I hit the light switch by my bed. I started to undress, peeling layers, remembering my time in the cold with Soames' body. The weather was tamer now so I wouldn't need to wear as much outside when I went later to bury him. But everything depended on when my mother turned in. Ordinarily she cleaned up the kitchen after dinner, watched a movie or a public television program in the living room, and retired by eleven. Tonight would be different, however, and I didn't know how long I'd have to sit listening to her say her piece to me. I'd have to wait till she did finish up and go to bed, and when I felt certain she was asleep, I'd get the shovel from the storeroom downstairs and march back out to the woods.

I heard the cellar door swing open. Here she came; she'd been down in her workshop, keeping busy at her pottery.

Footsteps on the stairs, the wood creaking, then her voice:

"Kurt, that you?"

"Who else would it be?"

She stopped in my doorway and stared at me, as stern and piercing in her look as a hawk.

"Mom…the smoke?"

Upturned by her chin, her weazened right hand, speckled with clay, was holding a cigarette.

"I've had better days than this one, Kurt…mind telling me where you disappeared to?"

"I took a little trip. Spur of the moment thing."

"A trip where?"

"Here we go. The questions."

"I'm only asking. I got up this morning and you weren't here, you don't show up all day."

"Relax. We'll work on the book tomorrow."

"It's not about that."

"Isn't it?"

"I'm only asking."

"The city, all right?"

"The city? Why?"

"I felt like it. Now I'm back and just in time for lockdown."

"You could've left a note," my mother said. "You could have called."

"I didn't think of it."

"I'm here smoking—"

"And eating grilled cheese sandwiches?"

"It's not funny. That's my comfort food. Something could happen to you and I wouldn't know where you are."

"Mom, your smoke's bugging me. Do I need to say it? You have two floors and the basement to smoke in. You can't leave this floor free?"

She hid the burning cigarette behind her back.

"Come downstairs. I have to tell you something."

"What?"

"Come down. I want to make coffee and I have something to tell you."

"Just tell me. If it's a speech—"

"It's not. But something strange happened and the police were here today."

I seated myself at the kitchen table while my mother got the coffee tin from the freezer. She fussed around at the large island counter, scooping the grounds into a filter. My head had been pulsing as we walked down the stairs, my heart kicking inside my chest, but I did what I could to appear unconcerned. I crossed one knee over the other and doodled with a finger on the tabletop.

"You want to make a cup for me?"

"I can."

My mother turned to the wall counter and put the filter in the coffee machine. It started to hum right after she pressed it on.

"Do you know anyone named Ralph Soames?"

She was facing me again, her elbows resting on the island counter.

"What's the name?"

"Ralph Soames."

I let a beat pass and gave a perfunctory shake of the head. "No. Should I?"

"How should I know?" my mother said. "But the police came here asking questions about him."

"What about?"

"He's missing."

"Is he somebody big or something? Important?"

"He's a dentist. Dentist or doctor. Which was it?... Dentist."

He'd been reported missing, the cops had told her, and last had been seen across the street in the graveyard.

"What was he doing there?"

"Kurt, I don't know the man. What do you do in a graveyard? Visit a grave."

All the water from the tank had dripped down into the coffee pot. My mother filled two cobalt-blue mugs and brought them to the table with two teaspoons. Neither of us took milk or cream.

"So I don't understand," I said, picking up the sugar dish. "What happened? The guy was last seen at the graveyard... and the cops came here, *why*?"

"They didn't tell me much. Something happened over there — an incident they said — and since then he's been missing."

"What kind of incident? When?"

"I told you, they didn't go into details. But it happened yesterday."

"It all seems..." I tried to find the appropriate words. "Pretty vague."

"No vaguer than you with your disappearance, going into the city on the spur of the moment."

"What's that mean — my disappearance? I'm here."

"You didn't take your car."

"I took the bus."

"The eleven-o-five?"

"The one-o-five."

"Hmm-hmm. Why wouldn't you? And dressed so rakishly."

I looked down at myself - white tennis shoes, dirt marks on my jeans, the red and black plaid shirt that had been underneath my sweat shirt. I was telling her that on a freezing night, at one a.m., I'd gotten the urge to take the bus into the city and to do it clad like a bum.

"Research," I said. "For a little thing I'm working on. My own piece. How the homeless survive the New York winters. I went undercover for a night."

But it sounded dubious even to me.

My mother had set the kitchen's lighting low. In her clay-streaked pottery smock over a blue-gray shirt and pants, she herself looked gray, indistinct in her chair, and the smoke from her cigarette added to that. I felt as if I was talking to a ghost, but the penetrating light in her eyes never wavered.

"I'm joking about the research," I said. "But I did go down to the city wearing this. No deep reason. I felt like getting out and going somewhere, taking a leisurely ride, and I didn't think to change. I just didn't feel like doing any driving."

Through the window I could see the black sky. I stared at the sky with my cup to my lips and thought about how I must sound. I couldn't explain my trip to New York credibly, but I hadn't been expecting such dire developments. The police inquiries — what was that? So soon after the event? Last seen in the graveyard? How could the cops know what had happened in the graveyard? Did they know? Fuck, I didn't even know what they knew.

I needed to ask a question.

"Why did the police come here anyway? How could we help them?"

My mother's brow furrowed. "If we'd seen or heard anything," she said, voice measured, edged with a wryness uncommon for her. "This is the only house nearby."

Last seen in the graveyard. By whom? What did the cops know? That Soames was dead? They wouldn't have described him as missing, would they, if they knew he'd been killed.

My mother kept her eyes on me while smoking her cigarette shorter and shorter, and I was reminded that this old woman, eccentric and tightly wound, wrapped up in herself and the writing of her book, was no fool. She'd been an attorney for thirty years, a Public Defender. She could read body language and changes in voice tone and had a keen feel for when people were lying. My story about why I'd gone to the city sounded untrue, and she had to have linked that puzzling trip to the appearance of the cops at our door and their report of a missing man.

I rose from my chair and feigned a yawn, trying to reveal nothing.

"Well, I'm beat. I'm turning in."

"The cops may stop back tomorrow," my mother said.

Our eyes met and I fought for calmness.

"If that's what they want. I can't tell them anything but—"

"They said they want to talk to you."

"They asked for me?"

"No…" She drew a last puff on her cigarette, let the smoke go, and mashed the butt out in the ashtray. "Or actually, yes, after talking to me. It's not like they came to talk to you, no. Didn't seem that way. But since you weren't home…"

"Where'd you tell them I was?"

"I didn't know, did I? Out drinking, in somebody's bed…"

"Not this time."

"So you say."

"What'd you tell them, mom?"

"I said you were out and I didn't know when you'd be back."

TWELVE

The talk over, I went up to my room and lit an aromatic candle. I lay down in bed with my sneakers off and my eyes trained on the ceiling. Hands beneath my head, I tried to use deep breathing techniques to get my pulse rate down. The jumping in my skin was causing disorder in my brain and I wanted to feel less frazzled so I could think lucidly. *Don't fold*, I thought. *That's the last thing you need. Pick it over. You have to dissect what she told you.*

First: Who, last night, might have seen Ralph Soames in the graveyard? Had someone been there besides myself and Catherine? I'd noticed no one, and if the person had seen Ralph Soames, they would have seen Catherine and possibly me. But the cops hadn't brought up Catherine to my mother (or she hadn't *told* me they had), and nothing she'd said led me to believe the cops thought I had been in the graveyard. So what the fuck? It didn't add up. It made no sense unless...

Catherine, myself, and Soames were in the graveyard - three people pursuing their obsessions in the twilight. What if nobody else was there? I didn't report him missing. And Soames is dead.

That leaves only one possibility. But why would Catherine speak to the cops?

I heard my mother on the second floor, running the water in her bathroom. At long last, she was preparing for bed and in an hour, when I knew she was asleep, I could go out to the woods. Alarming shit might be happening here, but I had to complete my business with the body. I had to dig Soames' grave and scrape away the dried blood in the tomb.

The smell of vanilla intensified, spreading out from the lit candle, and I kept grappling with the question of whether Catherine had called the police. I didn't want to think she had, but unless there'd been a fourth person in the graveyard, the caller must have been her. But again, why? To give herself up? When Soames had entered the tomb, interrupting her in whatever she was doing, she'd screamed at him with demoniacal anger. Then in some way he'd ended up dead — from a push by her, as I saw it. Had she felt regret later and informed the cops? If so, it had been much later, because his body had still been lying there at three o'clock that night.

But the cops say he's missing. Not murdered, missing. Which I guess makes sense if they don't have his body.

I decided to stop tormenting myself and do what was in my power to do — bury Soames. I'd get that done then come back for the cleaning products to scrub away the blood in the tomb. When the cops came tomorrow, if they came, I'd see what they had to say.

I didn't go out for another two hours, waiting till I was sure my mother was asleep. I took the shovel from the storeroom and a pair of gardening gloves and wore clothes lighter than last night's. A fine rain had started to fall, creating the thinnest of mist, and as I circumvented the graveyard, I looked over at the white tomb. *This is sick*, Soames had yelled before he died. *I'd like an explanation.* But what had he seen Catherine doing? Could it really be necrophilia? I didn't see how because June Hazzard's coffin was shut tight. Had to be masturbation, some autoerotic act. Coward. I'd stood there in the vault in one room, listening to her groans from the back room, and I'd never dared push open the door between them. If I had, would she have got violent with me also?

Flashlight on, defying the mist, I ploughed ahead through the increasing rain. If it kept up like this, I'd get drenched to the bone, but it seemed, too, like a stroke of luck because it might loosen the soil. I'd have to make the grave of adequate depth to insure that the body stayed buried, and I was concerned about how hard the digging was going to be.

I walked the half mile down the path through the woods and turned after ducking at the low-hanging branch. The grayness had thickened, reducing the effectiveness of my light, but I knew I was near the fallen oak. I could hear the stream's gurgling current. I came out on the bank, where it was mossy, and after I'd looked left and right, I saw the oak not ten yards away.

I'd worn no hat nor a coat with a hood. And without tree cover, I felt how the rain had the hardness of ice. I wiped away water rolling down my forehead and plunged the shovel into the dirt so that the handle stayed upright, then went over to the oak and knelt, my flashlight aimed beneath the trunk.

Soames wasn't there.

I blinked when I saw this, blinked and laughed, and I rubbed my eyes with my fingers as if they were playing tricks on me. But my second look confirmed my first.

The body was gone.

Can't happen, I thought. *Soames is dead. One hundred per cent rigor mortis dead and the dead don't get up and walk away.*

The sound of the rain was all around me, hitting the branches, dirt, and stream. The mist was cold and clammy on my face, my clothes were sopping, and a bar had spread across my chest, paralyzing my breathing. I had a moment where I doubted my sanity, wondered whether I'd dreamt the preceding night and never brought Soames' body out here. But no, I knew I'd hidden it under the oak and knew that in this rain and fog I could do nothing. It'd be futile to comb the area; I'd be flailing about like a blind man. Something had happened to the corpse, something had moved it, but I couldn't imagine what.

Think. Don't panic. Think. A dog. An animal maybe. A hungry wild dog came across it.

Or a person

I stood, I spun, I grabbed the shovel. I got myself back to the path. My lungs were operating again but all of a sudden my head hurt. Pain sawed at my temples.

I know these fucking woods, I thought, *and if the body's here, I'll find it.*

THIRTEEN

I rose around ten with rheumy eyes. A dry soreness was in my throat. My exploits last night had brought on a cold and the weather today didn't cheer me up. Outside my window the sky was gray, the pane itself striped with water. I looked across the road and over at the tomb where Ralph Soames had breathed his last, and for the first time since his death I had the thought that Catherine Embers might never come back to visit.

If he's dead, my brain's voice told me. *If he wasn't alive when you put him in the woods.*

I walked down to the kitchen and took the orange juice carton from the fridge. My mother, dressed already, was drinking coffee and reading the *Times*, a cigarette in the ashtray by her hand.

"Ten thirty," I said. "I'm surprised you didn't wake me to start at sunrise."

"Very funny."

"I can hope. You finishing the book yourself? Am I fired?"

"You don't get off that easy," my mother said, flipping a page of the newspaper.

"I don't know. I hate every minute I'm working on the thing but I can't seem to pull myself away from it."

"Look..." She closed the section of the paper she'd been reading and put it folded on the table. "We'll do some more later today or tomorrow."

"Good to see you're loosening up."

"I'm not. I don't want any more interruptions though and if the cops come today...see what they want, talk to them, and we'll get back to it."

She took herself off to her basement workshop and the day for me became an agony of waiting. Over coffee, an apple, and oat bran donuts, I read all the sections of the *New York Times*. I went up to my room and put on a CD of Scheherazade and lay down in bed to listen. The rain had stopped, though the sky hadn't brightened, and I was dying to go into the woods and do a search for Soames' body. In daylight, I'd be able to see out there. If the body was near where I'd stashed it, I'd recover and bury it. Unless Soames was alive and had walked away...but I didn't believe this possible. When I'd touched him, when I'd carried him, he'd been stiff with rigor mortis. That was definite. I hadn't imagined his condition. He'd been meat, and something else, human or otherwise, had moved him. I had to keep reminding myself of this to expel irrational thoughts. The thoughts would infiltrate my mind and I'd see Ralph Soames tearing out of the woods, running across the road to our house, beating at the door while calling my name and promising vengeance.

The doorbell rang at five of two. From the kitchen, where I was brewing tea for my throat, I'd heard a car turn into our driveway, and when I looked through the window over the sink, I saw a blue police car. One man got out, in dun brown pants and a blue-black jacket, a trooper's hat on his head, and I let him mosey up the walkway before going over to the door.

"Who's that, Kurt?"

My mother was standing on the top cellar step, behind me down the hall.

"The police officer."

"Just one?"

"Yes."

"There were two yesterday."

"If he wants you, I'll shout."

After he rang the bell a second time, I opened the door.

Preliminaries established that he was one of the two who'd come yesterday and that I was the person who'd been out when they came.

"Would you like some tea?" I asked him.

"No thanks."

"Well, I'm making some — I gotta cold — so let's go into the kitchen."

At the table, over that cup of tea with lemon, I tried to appear uninformed and give the policeman neutral answers. Though he was seeking information from me, I wanted to draw something about the case out of him. Nothing doing: he covered only what he and the other cop had told my mother the day before. A man, Ralph Soames, a dentist, had last been seen two evenings ago in the graveyard across the street. He'd arrived in his car and since that time both he and the car, a silver Jaguar, had been missing. His receptionist had come in to work yesterday morning and today, but she hadn't heard anything from him. She'd cancelled appointments with his clients. This woman had been in his employ for years and the word she had for him was "ultra-responsible". He'd never take off and leave others in the lurch.

"Is he married?" I asked.

"No wife. No kids."

"Jeesh. You can't ever tell with people."

The photo he'd handed me of Soames, a color headshot, was next to my cup.

"And you're sure you've never seen this man?"

I looked at the photo again, neither overdoing a concentrating face nor trying to seem blase.

"I haven't. No." I lifted my teacup. "Did he come to the cemetery often?"

"He'd been there before. That's what we think."

The policeman was hard to size up; under his hat his mustached face looked positively genial. But despite his pleasantness, I had the impression that he knew more than he was letting on. Did the cops have a lead? I assumed they'd questioned the attendants who cared for the graveyard. And they were speaking to me and my mother because we lived by the place and might have seen or heard something. What I couldn't fit together was why they were on the case so promptly. Soames, this officer had said, had last been seen two evenings earlier. That was less than two days ago. Yet by yesterday afternoon they'd been inquiring into his "disappearence." This all for an ordinary dentist? An adult of sound mind and body? Either Soames held a position of importance I knew nothing about or the police had reason to believe a crime had occurred. Had they seen the bloodstains in the tomb? They very well might have. Shaken last night that the body was gone, I'd forgotten all about cleaning up the blood, and anyhow, if Catherine had been the person to tell them something had happened to Soames, they might have examined the tomb and blood as early as the morning after the incident. It still seemed nutty, but the woman I was breaking the law to help may have given the police their lead.

"If you don't mind my asking...is this guy only a dentist?"

"*Only* a dentist?" the policeman said.

"He's been gone, you said, two days. Isn't that fast to call someone missing? I mean, if he's the mayor of the town or something..."

"Not at all, not at all. He's a dentist in Kingston, like I told you. But we think something might've happened to him, yes."

"I see. In the graveyard?"

"Perhaps."

"Weird."

I rose to wash out my teacup and the policeman stood up with me. His face remained smiley under his wide-brimmed hat.

"If I'd seen anything..." I said, rinsing my cup in the sink. "But I haven't. Sorry."

"Thanks anyway. Glad to have caught you. Your mother said you're usually here in the afternoons."

"Usually."

"And this is where you live. With her?"

"Uh-huh. I'm helping her write a book."

"You're a writer?"

"Sadly enough."

"If you remember anything, anything you might've noticed..."

"I'll let you know."

He gave me a card with his name and work number on it, and I saw him to the door.

"Is she home, your mother?"

"Downstairs. Should I get her?"

"That's all right. Thanks again for your time."

I closed the door but stayed by the window beside it, watching through the curtain as his car left the driveway. All those final questions he'd asked. Did I live here with my mother? Wasn't I usually home in the afternoons? He'd come yesterday and seen her and not me; in calling today he'd seen me but not her. What did he think was at play here — a Tony Perkins-like switcheroo out of *Psycho*? Gimme a break. I may have problems, I thought, but I'm no Norman Bates.

FOURTEEN

My mother came upstairs and saw me fretting by the window. Wet plaster was on her hands, a clay splotch on her face. She had a green kerchief tied around her neck.

"What?" I said.

"Are you done?"

"Seems so."

"What'd he ask?"

"What he asked you more or less."

"No questions about where you were yesterday?"

My back tensed. "Why would he?"

"No reason. I didn't tell him you were out the night before so as far as he knows you were just gone for the afternoon."

"And by that you mean?"

"Nothing."

She pushed out her face and put a look on it, egging me to coax her on.

"I'll bite, ma. You think because I went out late at night and the cops show up the next day, I was doing something I shouldn't?"

"Did I say that?"

She was down the hall in the cellar doorway, her steely gray eyes cutting into me again. Then she turned her head and I was looking at her in profile — the aquiline nose, the slim-lipped mouth, the hard stamp of her jaw. She had never more resembled a bird of prey.

"Why'd you go out on a freezing night at two in the morning? Fair question. And come back all dirty, giving me some cockamamie story about riding the bus to the city..."

"I did go down to the city," I said.

"And on the same night a man nearby disappears. Who can tell? Could be coincidence."

"I have a cold. I'm goin' up to take a nap."

"I thought we'd work on the book."

"Let's make it tomorrow."

"We missed yesterday also."

"I said tomorrow. Can't you do any writing yourself? Draft the next section for me to start from?"

"I'll hold you to tomorrow," my mother said. "No later than ten. We have to get back on schedule."

My mother seemed to think I was mixed up in everything. News flash, I was, but what did she think I'd done? Murder? And why hadn't she mentioned her suspicions to the police? So long as I restarted work on her book, my other activities were unimportant. I could be out killing people, for all she cared, if I kept writing her autobiography.

Write, write, write. Fuck me. Why didn't I just drop the fucking thing?

I will, I thought. Maybe. But first things first.

Tonight I had to find that body.

FIFTEEN

I went out before it got dark. I felt low already with my sore throat and congested nose, and my bad mood blackened as I hiked to the stream bank. My daily walk, as far as my mother knew, my exercise and nothing more. But why the fuck was I doing this? For what reward, what payoff? I was risking arrest to help Catherine Embers but I was invisible to her. No, beyond that. A guardian angel she didn't even know she had. I was busting my hump to keep her from police detection, yet she may have told the police what she did. Screwy, the whole situation, deranged.

Despite the breezes high and low, bending the tree tops, turning over leaves, the air for the second straight day was warm. About fifty, parka warm. And a breeze it was, manna from heaven, that tipped me off to the body's location. Standing by the oak where I'd rammed Soames's corpse, I was looking for signs of disturbance in the dirt — footprints, paws, anything — when a smell collided with my face and my stomach rushed up to my throat. I covered my mouth with my hand. But nothing inside me came out and, in fact, I was smiling. The smell was like maggoty meat, the unambiguous smell of putrescence.

Bingo, I thought.

I followed, as they say, my nose. Let it guide me away from the stream and over to where the tree line started. The wind seemed to shift and I lost the scent but by then I didn't need the wind because I saw two black shoes. Saw them about ten feet in front of me — muddied shoes with their toe ends up. The black trousers had rips everywhere, the skin beneath was a bloodless white. Pieces of Soames' arms were gone, all his fingers, his heart and chest. No Sherlock Holmes was needed to tell me that a creature had fed on him, but whatever had used him as a midwinter feast had spared chowing down on his face. That was ashen but unmarked, and under his frozen dirty-blonde hair he had the same sterile expression I'd seen him with when he was alive.

"My apologies, Soames."

Did my words alert the creature? Or my smell? Or had it been watching me from nearby? I heard a bark and stirring behind me and I think I rotated in the air to see what beast I'd intruded on.

A dog. Rather, a wolf! Something canine, black, and mangy — after I laid eyes on the thing, I didn't stand there to classify it. The dog charged while growling at me and the fight or flight instinct triggered, a mechanism that requires no thought.

I know I ran with the dog at my heels. I know I slapped at branches. I sprinted without seeing till halted by the stream, and when I stopped, thought returned. I got my bearings. I could still hear the dog, but I'd lengthened the distance between us. *Was* it a wolf? It had the snout, body, and pointy ears of one, that bushy fur, but neither the height nor the bulk. I realized too that whatever it was the creature had something wrong with it. From what I saw, a hitch marred its gait. Its steps were hops and its head kept ducking, and as it limped through the bushes toward me, I could see where the problem lie.

The dog had a leg that never touched the ground, a crippled leg, pawless.

Quick as a flash, my fright waned. It didn't die, just shaded into anger. I felt this anger building up, rage at each and every frustration I'd been having these past months. I thought of the shit I always thought about — my mother's book, my own aborted projects, my laughable sex life and obsession with Catherine, the works — and I couldn't accept that to go with all that I had to fight a fucking dog. A rickety, crazed three-legged cur I had to get past to bury Soames. In that extended moment, as I held my ground, as I raised my arms to defend myself, the animal became a living symbol for my entire malformed existence. Fucked-up man, lame man. That in a nutshell is Mr. Kurt Morgan. I wanted to grip its emaciated throat and strangle it to death while biting its eyes out.

I didn't do that. But I did scan the ground for a weapon, a stone or stick I could use to hit it. The dog stopped, sniffing me, searching for the odor of fear to return, and from this came a primeval stare-down across the moist dirt of the stream bank. Man and animal facing off, eyes unblinking, retreat or attack. Three steps forward and I could've kicked the dog like a football; one leap (if it could leap) and it would've been going for *my* throat.

"Get lost. You ate your fill."

Graveyard Love

But the dog had found its treasure. Meat to last for awhile. And a dog with a useless leg, constrained in what it could do to forage, was not about to give that up. I tried again, talking to it, using a low unthreatening voice, hoping the dog had once been a pet and would warm up when spoken to gently, but I got answered by a baring of teeth and a mindless rabid growl.

I broke to my left; it jumped. I saw bloodlust in its eyes. I dropped to one knee as the dog went flying over my head, and as I rose, I heard a splash. The dog had landed in the stream and I went scrambling up the bank to seize a dead branch on the ground.

In the swift current, the dog was thrashing. Its tongue hung out. But I was not sympathetic, my idea to clout it when it reached the bank. It writhed and paddled across the current, and when it hauled itself onto the bank, I put my loose hand on the branch. I gave a Herculean swing. My blow caught the dog on the side of the head and it barked once, whimpered with pain. But it kept charging hop by hop, and I had to strike the dog again. I struck with an overhead blow, a caveman thwack to its cranium. Blood flew from its ear. Even that didn't squelch the fight in it, though, and the dog made another attempt for my throat, springing upwards. I thrust my stick straight out and speared the animal in the belly. It squealed like a hog. I watched it go sailing back into the water and splash down with a plop, redness spreading. It did not come up.

I'm going, I thought. *To her. After this, I have to. Fuck yes. I'll tell her what happened, tell her everything I've done for her sake. From the body, to his car, to this demonic animal...She can do what she wants when she hears, she can think me a creep and send for the cops, but I have to go.*

I could see it already. An original way to introduce myself. Ring her bell, speak when she opened the door. *Hi. Catherine? I'm Kurt. I've watched you for a long time and you have to hear what I've done for you. The risks I've taken. I've gone above and beyond for you. Nobody else would've done these things. Nobody. I'm the guy who took the trouble to bury the man you killed.*

Mind if I come in?

I left the house later with my flashlight and a shovel. When I got to Soames' body, I tied an old shirt over my face.

The burial itself? A spartan one.

No prayers, no tributes, no ceremony.

Just smells.

SIXTEEN

I did my writing through the day, waited till evening, then drove to her house. I foresaw armor and various defenses, a guarded human being, and I had no strategy to break her down. But when she opened her front door, I blurted out two words.

"Ralph Soames."

Abrupt start, like I'd thrown a brick, and I watched Catherine take a short step backwards

"Excuse me?"

"Ralph Soames. He—"

She had on no make-up and I could see the lines in her face. Crow's feet at the corners of her eyes. The color of her eyes was a darkish green, and from up this close her cheekbones looked movie star striking. They were that wide and that high, though the coarseness in their structure, as in her mouth, still made it a stretch to call her pretty.

"I'm sorry," I said. "I'll start again."

"You're not the police."

"Me? No. Nothing to do with the police."

"Then you are...?"

"Kurt Morgan. There's a reason Ralph Soames is missing."
"Who's Ralph Soames?"
"I buried him in the woods for you. He won't be found."
"What is this?"
"I know what happened," I said. "But it's okay. I'm not here to make threats or demands. I...Here. Read this."

Last night I'd decided that to write what I'd been doing, how I'd been watching her, would be easier than telling her everything. She could digest the information alone, at her own speed. But I wanted her to see where the letter came from, to put the writing to a face. Now I had to hope she didn't call the cops.

"My cell number's there. And my address. Or you can find me sometimes at the Fieldhouse Tavern."

Light pink freckles were in her skin and her hair today was done in a braid snaking down to the middle of her back.

Can I touch it? I thought. *Can I kiss your hair?*

"Your name's what again?"
"Kurt Morgan."
"Wait here."
"It's a long letter. Why don't you call me...?"
"Wait."

She withdrew with the envelope and banged the door closed. Weak in the knees, I walked down her stoop and over toward her driveway, my car. It seemed that I'd botched the introduction and that Catherine would run straightaway to the phone. The police would find me here, a docile stalker hoping for her love. Maybe she thought I intended blackmail. My letter explained that I wanted no money, nothing like that, but how could she not consider me a danger? She would have to, I thought, anyone would if I came to them as I had to her, but there was no avoiding that. First contact, I'd known, would be bumpy. It might result in my arrest. But I'd made the vow to reach out to her and I was prepared for whatever might follow.

If I could touch her hair, I thought. *The long red hair. If I could go inside while she's reading the letter, walk up from behind her at her table, lower my mouth, kiss her hair while she reads...*

I waited in my car listening to Bartok, his Concerto for Orchestra, and unexpected questions occupied my head. They were issues I'd refrained from thinking about before. What did Catherine do for money? How did she pay for her house? I'd driven by the place in the morning, the afternoon, night, and most every time her Nissan was in her driveway. She had no garage. The one-floor house, triangular-roofed, was nothing fancy, but she had to have an income from somewhere. Did she work at home?

The Bartok piece ended, evening also. The sky was black and the moon hidden by clouds. It had been an hour since I'd given her the letter, and though it was lengthy, five handwritten pages, she should've read it through in half that time. I must be deluded, I said to myself. Utterly gone. She's not coming out.

An acute despair took me in its grip, hopelessness almost suicidal. I felt I might put my head through the windshield. It was that or drive off alone through the night, and the second option I couldn't face. An hour ago, I'd been willing to drop my letter off and leave; not now. Where would I go? I'd drink myself silly if I went to a bar, and back home in my room, I'd feel so lonely it would be unbearable.

Come out and give me a sign. A hint of what you think. Catherine.

The car had gotten cold, so I put on the engine and ran the heat. I didn't smash my head through the windshield. But I stayed parked in Catherine's driveway, nose to tail with her Nissan. I was sniffling and coughing and had the warm woozy feeling of a fever, but I was limiting my drugs to aspirin. I did have my flask, loaded with brandy, and fished that from my jacket for a swig. Then I rolled back my seat and closed my eyes.

Repeated taps on the window awoke me. It's what made me aware I'd fallen asleep. I sat up straight as if I'd been yanked and there was Catherine's face at the driver's side window, unsmiling, green eyes hard. She'd swathed herself in her shiny black cloak and her hair was still tied in a braid.

"I'm gonna get in," she informed me. "We'll go over."

I had to stifle an involuntary yawn and allow myself time for my head to clear.

"Over?" I said. "Where?"

"To the cemetery."

"Hold it. I don't—"

"I'll come round. You can drive."

"The cemetery. Your cemetery?"

"We'll do it in the tomb."

"June Hazzard's tomb?"

I must've sounded dim, with my echoing questions.

"You know where that is Kurt, right? Am I right?"

She knew she was, and once she got in, I put the car into reverse.

There were no lamp posts along her street and I drove through the darkness carefully. Heat from the vents permeated the car. The Bartok disc had begun again - I shut the music off. When I'd glance at Catherine, she'd break out in a smile, but the smiles possessed irony alone, bewildering me. *A joke is in progress,* that look said, but I couldn't tell who Catherine was saying the joke was on. Me or her. Whoever she meant, her eyes retained their grimness.

A green-eyed killer, I thought, and the phrase, though redolent of pulp fiction, seemed apt.

Catherine had iced one man in the tomb; I'd go next. Was that the reason for the smile? "Soames was last seen in the graveyard," I said. "The police know that. I'm not sure how, but they do. But they don't know what happened to him next, if he's dead or off somewhere. That's what they led me to think."

"When?"

"Yesterday."

"They came to your house?"

"Yeah. Before I buried him."

"Did they mention me?"

"No. Have they—? They've spoken to you already?"

"How do I know you did bury Soames?" Catherine asked. "You have proof?"

"I'll show you where."

"Where's he buried?"

"Yeah. He's there and I put in his wallet and the papers from his car, everything."

"Thorough."

"Had to be. Want me to show you?"

"What for?" Catherine said. "I believe you."

She gave me the ironic smile again but something now was added to it. One side of her mouth went up higher than the other and the asymmetry brought a new quality to her face, something I hadn't seen before. Hardness had transformed into weary resignation, submission to a fate that must be endured.

It's the killing, I thought. *She doesn't want to kill me but feels she must. She's gotten tired of having to knock off these intrusive men.*

Perhaps in the tomb, she'd pull a knife from under her cloak. Or take out a gun. I didn't put either past Catherine; she seemed unperturbed that the cops were on the Ralph Soames case, snooping around. She might try to make me victim number two, and if that happened, I'd defend myself. I wasn't hoping to die tonight. But having unveiled myself to her, having laid myself bare at last, I couldn't turn back and drive her home. Come what may, in this dance we were doing, I'd let her lead and react to that. I'd see the night through to its denouement, I decided.

SEVENTEEN

Between our driveway and the gravel by the cemetery gate, I chose to park in the driveway. At the same time, I worried that my mother, if she was in the kitchen or her bedroom, would see me getting out of the car with Catherine. She'd have to wonder what in hell was going on if she saw us cross the road and walk into the graveyard. To her it was the graveyard Ralph Soames had vanished from on the night I'd gone AWOL. And speaking of suspicions, what about the police? Was it safe for Catherine and me to go into June Hazzard's tomb? The cops, in the shed by the graveyard entrance, might have it under surveillance.

Catherine had opened her door and gotten out. She was looking around. I stood waiting by my door.

"The house with the eyes in the windows," Catherine said.

"My eyes," I said. "Nobody else's."

"I never noticed anything all these months."

"Ralph Soames seemed to."

"He never told me he did."

"When he came over that night...Christ! How did he suss me out?"

"He might've seen you sometime," Catherine said. "All your following us around."

"He did but you didn't?"

"Why not? Maybe it didn't click with him till you called."

"I fucked that up. Got too cute."

"Something you said told him."

Catherine motioned with her head.

"You have two cars?"

"Two? No. That's my mother's."

"What's her car doing here?"

"It's her house."

"You didn't tell me that," she said. "That you live with someone."

"I don't," I said. "Live with someone. It's my mother. Does that qualify as living with someone?"

A look approximating a smile, dry amusement, came and went on Catherine's face.

"Maybe not," she said. "But that's funny."

"Up there..." I pointed. "On that side of the house. That's my room."

"I can't see the telescope."

"It's away from the window, on a stand."

"What does mommy think you have it there for?"

"Astronomy," I said. "What else?"

"Observing mourners. Spying on people in their most painful moments of grief."

"I don't do that."

"No. Why would you?"

She said this sarcastically and shook her head and I thought I saw whimsy flit through her eyes. If she asked for an invite in, she knew, I'd squirm. My defensiveness talking about my mother must have betrayed that.

"She doesn't see anybody. She's a hermit."

"Who is?"

"My mother."

"What do I care?"

"Oh…"

"I don't want to meet her, Kurt. We may as well do what we have to do."

If she was planning to kill me, she seemed to assume I'd follow her like a doting lamb. And I did fall in behind her, moving down the driveway, across the road, and through the cemetery gate, passing the gravestones and crosses.

"Wait here. I have to light a candle."

I stopped at the mouth of the square white vault while Catherine went ahead into the darkness.

"Okay. You can come in."

A candle was burning on the slab where Soames had hit his head. This was in the front room. But Catherine had slipped into the second, and she hadn't closed the door between the two

"Come on," she said. "No secrets now."

I stepped through the doorway, my nerves on the highest alert.

"She's back here, underneath stone, but she won't let me go."

Catherine's voice sounded weary. Her hand touched my arm. She was standing beside me and she'd lit white candles on the white sarcophagus inscribed with the name June Hazzard.

"How do you want to do it?"

"Do what?" I said.

"You're not gonna play coy, are you? That's so not what I want."

We were staring eye to eye, but somewhere between our mouths spoken words were going astray. Catherine seemed to expect something from me and I didn't have a clue what it was.

"Catherine. You read my letter, you know how I feel about you, but I'm not sure why I'm here."

"Cut the shit and do it."

"Do what?"

"These head games are tedious."

"Did you tell the cops Ralph Soames is missing? No one else was in the graveyard that night."

"You *are* dedicated to watching me."

"You're not answering my question."

"I told the cops. That was me."

"Why? Fuck! Why?"

"I can't fight June. I'm tired of trying."

"June Hazzard?"

"I told them to turn myself in. To get my punishment. But obviously that isn't what she wants."

"Wants? She's dead."

"She wants everything from me — the ultimate price."

"Why are you talking like she's still alive?"

"Can we get this done already? Here. Use this."

She reached into her cloak and a knife appeared. It must've had a blade of six or seven inches and I didn't object when she placed its brown leather handle in my hand.

"Catherine…" I felt stunned. "What do you want me to do?"

"Are you a sadist? Do it already."

"Spell it out."

"What's better? For me to lay out on her coffin? I'll lay my head down on the edge." On her knees, cheek to stone, Catherine Embers waited beneath me, and I looked down at her long braid. I could scalp her, I thought, peel the hair from her head, and keep her red tresses forever.

"I don't want to hurt you, Catherine."

"Use the knife like an ax. The guillotine."

"I'm not going to do that."

She rose mumbling curses, her cloak swishing, and her face went from white and freckled to a flaming red.

"What hole did you crawl from?"

"You know who I am."

"The hell I do. You're Kurt Morgan. So? You've been sneaking around, spying on me…What more do I know?"

"I—"

"You've been watching me, clocking my every move, cleaning up after me. If it's not to kill me, then why?"

I didn't answer.

"You're in love? You're demented enough to think that?"

"Catherine—"

"Or is this about wanting to fuck me?"

"If you'd let me talk…"

"It's not gonna happen," she said. "Not here, not anywhere."

She slumped to her knees again, her forehead pressed to June Hazzard's coffin, and she made a noise like a person choking. Her shoulders were trembling and her fingernails clawed at the marble. As I stood over her, the knife in my hand, her choking erupted into sobs, and the sobs became louder and louder...

Sobs of anguish, reverberating inside the tomb.

PART TWO

EIGHTEEN

As if to put us all through hell, a sweep of polar air hit, restoring the brutal cold. The temperature sank below zero and stayed there, night, morning, and day. No snow fell but the wind cut like razors and dissuaded me from going out. Even my walks I put on hold. My mother, a veteran of upstate winters, had two huge refrigerators and knew to keep them well-stocked for when these nasty bouts came. So with meat, fish, and water at the ready, coffee for a month, cigarette cartons in the freezer and canned goods stuffing our pantry, we had no need to go anywhere. My mother and I had a bunker. Just as well for her: confined to the house, I had no excuse not to forge ahead with the book. I wrote seven hours a day. My mother saw this and liked; she didn't bring up the night I'd gone AWOL or the cops' investigation. She didn't go overboard with edits. I got into a rhythm and the pages accumulated. We had entered her college years, fun times at Columbia. The late sixties. I'm sure my mother was hoping the cold spell would last till I completed the book. Meantime, I didn't hate doing the writing because it kept my brain occupied. By occupied, I mean off Catherine. I didn't know how to move forward on that front.

For starters, there was her ingratitude. Not a word of thanks had come from her. No acknowledgement that I'd cleaned up her mess. After her histrionics in the tomb, she ordered me to take her home, but then she clammed up during the ride. She sat with her face to the passenger window and didn't speak till I reached her driveway.

"Don't come ringing my bell," she said. "Don't phone."

"And that's it?"

"What else is there?"

"An explanation."

"I don't know you and I don't want to know you."

She pulled the door latch, opened the door, swung her legs outside.

"Stalk me anymore and you'll be sorry."

"Is that a threat?"

"Don't do it."

Was she displeased *because* I'd removed Soames' body? If she'd called the cops to turn herself in, saying she'd killed the guy, then my interference had defeated her purpose. They couldn't pin a charge on her if the person she claimed to have killed had vanished. No body, no crime. But what, please, had her breakdown in the tomb been about? And why had she thought I'd take her life?

I've never liked a woman who's sane, I thought. *Can't be any other way, can it?*

NINETEEN

The invite came out of the blue, Catherine phoning, asking to meet. It was ten twenty-five at night, and I could hear noise around her, talking and music. I didn't know quite what to say.

"Don't you want to see me?" Catherine asked.

"Yes, but—"

"Then get over here. The Fieldhouse Tavern. I'm on my second but you can catch up."

Nothing about why she desired my company now, but whatever the reason, I felt I had to go. Couldn't let this opportunity pass.

From inside my room, my mother must have heard me leave (if she did, too bad) and my car started quickly despite the cold. I saw Catherine on a bar stool when I walked in, but before I could sit on the one beside her, she gestured toward the back area, the booths and tables there.

"More private," she said. "Better to talk."

The jukebox was playing Elvis Costello and a Knicks game was on the TV. I ordered a Myer's and Coke from Tony and put out a five dollar bill, and Catherine asked for another screwdriver. As we walked to the back, heads swiveled, eyes watched us; I could feel the envy. Every guy in that place wanted to fuck Catherine and had imagined himself doing it, but each knew he had no chance. Most had abandoned the humble ambition of striking a conversation with her. She wants no part of us loser males, the thinking went, but if that was so, why was she talking to me tonight, a fellow loser? Why huddle in a booth with that guy? I was wondering myself, considering everything, but I was tickled she'd given the regulars something to yak about.

"I'm surprised you want to see me," I said.

"I want to say something," Catherine said. "Something I'm not happy about."

"What?"

"You fucked things up for me royally."

"If you mean the cops."

"I can't go back to June's tomb when I know you're watching."

"I haven't been watching. I—"

"That's all you've done, pervert. Watch."

"That was before. The last week, no."

"You sitting there by your telescope."

"I put it away."

"Why don't I believe you?"

"I have. I promise."

She was wearing jeans and a green and white sweater with a high neck. I didn't see her black cloak but a black down jacket she'd thrown down beside her in the booth. Her hair hung free past her shoulders and an alcoholic flush was already visible in her face. The flush gave her a seductive radiance, and the lines around her eyes smoothed out.

"I'm still too sober for this," she said. "To talk to you."

"You called me."

"I know I did. But I need to likker up more first."

We finished that round and did another, then did two tequila shots with lime. She'd stare across the table at me or sag back in the booth, eyes closed, listening to the jukebox music. She made selections on it herself - songs by Joan Jett, Lucinda Williams, 4 Non Blondes. She picked one by Sade. Interesting range of choices, I thought, when she told me what she'd chosen. And she asked me if I liked Abba.

"Abba? Boy! I hated them when I was younger."

"So did I." A flicker of a smile.

"So mushy, yucky."

"But now," she said.

"I have to admit...yeah. As you get older, they sound okay."

"They write good songs. Songs that get to you."

"I wouldn't figure you for an Abba person," I said.

"I'm not an Abba person. I like their songs."

"Fair enough."

"Lemme guess. You took me for a Goth music chick."

"I never thought about it. What your tastes are. But someone who I always see in black, visiting a graveyard... You do seem pretty dark."

"You don't know me, Kurt."

"I realize that."

I didn't have to add she'd asked me to kill her. Putting labels aside, she *was* dark. But tonight she seemed to have no suicidal designs.

"I can see you wanna ask me questions."

"Is that so strange?" I said. "You were talking like June Hazzard's alive."

"I'm getting a buzz finally."

"Another shot?"

"No. But I'll take another screwdriver."

I walked to the bar and got one more for her and a Myer's and Coke for me.

"So, yeah." I slid back into the booth. "I do have a shitload of questions."

"And I have some for you."

"About what? Ask away. I'm open."

"How long have you been watching me?"

"I told you in my note. About six months."

"Six months. Six months..."

Her voice trailed off and she put her head down on the table, resting her chin on her folded hands, shutting her eyes as if she wanted to sleep. In such repose she looked untroubled, and I fought an electric urge to kiss her.

"It's like I wrote. I saw you on one of my walks and—"

"Became obsessed," she said, eyes still closed. "Crazy mad obsessed."

"Not right away. And I don't know. You make me sound like a dangerous nut."

"Aren't you?" She'd opened her eyes, raised her head.

"I don't think of myself as one, no."

Catherine shot to her feet, reached down for her glass, and tossed back her screwdriver. I could see her throat rippling as she drank. Then she slammed the glass down and looked at me, making a circling movement with her hand.

"Drink up. I wanna go somewhere."

"Where?" I said. "What time is it?"

"Two. Three. Your house."

"My house?"

"I wanna see the room you watch me from."

"We can't go there," I said.

"Let's see this telescope."

"We can't."

"Why not?"

"You don't want to, trust me."

"Is it momma? She forbids visitors."

"Fuck no."

"Then let's go," she said. "But let me ask you something first. How often do you jerk off, Kurt?"

"What?"

"How often?"

"You can't ask that."

"But you can spy on me. Follow me. That's okay."

"I won't answer that," I said.

"Do you have a girlfriend?"

"What do you think?"

"You getting any? From anyone?"

"I think I should leave."

"You're an onanist," Catherine said. "I have a feeling. I like that word. On-an-ist."

"I don't even know what that means."

"Yes, you do," she said. "Let's go to your house."

For sex? I thought. *To fuck? Could she be that drunk?* A week ago she'd spoken as if that was something forever out of the question between us.

"Why don't we go to yours?" I said.

"I wanna see your room. Yours. You gonna tell me you haven't jerked off thinking about having me alone in there?"

"If you have a fit like the other night..."

"I didn't have a fit."

"Whatever you call asking me to kill you."

"I made a misjudgment," Catherine said, dropping her eyes. "That won't happen again."

She grabbed her jacket and left the booth, swaying as she walked toward the bar's front door.

"You shouldn't be driving," I called out to her.

"Neither should you," she said. "Let's go."

TWENTY

I unlocked the front door, groped for the light switch. The pink-yellow bulb in the ceiling came on. Catherine walked in and saw the paintings in the front room, the amorphous dreamscapes my mother's father had done in Morocco. On a mantelpiece were blue and gold tea glasses from there, and I watched Catherine fingering them and the sheesha pipes beside them.

"Where have we gone? Casablanca?"

"Here's looking at you, kid."

"Obviously. That's your hobby."

I couldn't stop myself from giggling. "We're talking too loud. Let's go upstairs."

We mounted in the dark and I told Catherine to keep her hand on the banister.

"I can't see a thing."

"Shush. Grab the back of my coat and hold it."

She did that, and we went up to the second floor, across the landing by mother's door, and up again to my room. I shut the door behind us.

"There. You can talk now."

"Won't she hear through the floor?"

"I'm not directly over her. I mean, if you don't bellow or anything. And she sleeps like a log once she's out."

"How can you live this way? *How* old are you?"

"Thirty-five."

"So you follow a woman around, live with your mother. Can anyone say serial killer?"

"If I wanted to hurt you...Christ. I would've when you begged me to."

Catherine looked away. I'd sat down at my desk and put on my lamp, and I asked her to sit also. "Make yourself at home," I said, indicating my blue recliner, but Catherine turned her back on me and took a step toward my bookcase. This ran the length of one wall, my DVDs filled the shelves along another.

"That's right, I like horror films. I suppose that adds to my creepiness."

Catherine left the shelves and went over to the window, taking in with her naked eye the view overlooking the road and graveyard.

"Told ya. No telescope."

"A man of his word."

'You still want to see it? It's in the closet."

"A guy thirty five living with his mother, spends hours at his window watching a woman because she's got long red hair..."

"It's more than your red hair," I said.

"I don't need to hear it," Catherine said, and she turned from the window, unzipping her jacket. She threw it on the bed but didn't sit down, explaining that standing she'd sober up faster.

"Whatever helps. But I have wine in my closet if you want something."

There she was in her green and white sweater and form-fitting jeans. In my room — Catherine Embers. I felt as if something I'd dreamt was happening. Catherine Embers was in my bedroom, and I asked myself whether I had to let her leave it. If not for my mother being in the house, I could keep Catherine here with me. Not hurt her, but immobilize her somehow. Restrict her to the house, the room, the bed… But then again, besides the inconvenience of my mother's presence, people had seen us leave the bar together.

"Something I don't understand," Catherine said.

"What's that?"

She put her left hand underneath her right elbow, her right hand underneath her chin. "What do you do with yourself?" she said. "When you're not watching me. You have a job? What's your mother do?"

"She's retired."

"And your father?"

"He died five years ago."

"Let me guess. You're unemployed."

"I'm doing something to help my mother."

"Something illegal?"

"No! Where'd that come from?"

"Your reticent tone."

"Are you going to sit down already?"

"I will," Catherine said. "But go on. What are you doing for her?"

"Helping her write a book, of all things. A memoir."

"A what?"

"Memoir. As in life story. Autobiography."

"I know what a memoir is," Catherine said. "Whose? Hers?"

"It's about her growing up in Morocco and coming to the States as a teenager — I don't want to get into it. Suffice it to say, she's difficult to work with and how I haven't strangled her yet...Who knows? But that's the gist of it. I'm a writer, idiotic me, and if I kill anyone it won't be you. It'll be my mother."

Catherine sat down on my bed, leaning forward from one edge.

"I need a smoke." She riffled through her jacket and took out a pack of Newports.

"Thanks for asking."

"Can I?"

"I don't allow my mother to smoke in here. But if you must, you must. I'll make an exception."

She struck a match, lit up. I told her to use the wine glass on my night table as an ashtray. Then she lay back on one elbow, legs stretched off the end of the bed, one knee bent over the other, and looked at me while she smoked.

"You write on that laptop?"

"I do."

"How far have you gotten in the book?"

"Far. About three-fourths through. But at the rate we're going—"

"It could take forever."

"Seems like."

"Why not just dump it? Leave the house?"

"I should," I said. "I've been on the verge."

"Is she paying you?"

"No. But I don't pay rent or anything. "

"You've got to be kidding."

"I got laid off in the City and—"

"If it's torture, quit."

"I can't."

"Because she'll throw you out? You're a grown man."

"I have nowhere else to go, one, and more importantly I feel that quitting would let her beat me. She'd have broken my will."

"It's a macho thing?"

"Stubbornness," I said. "I promised I'd finish and it's become like a point of honor."

"Why don't you let me read what you have?"

"Come again?"

"Let me run through it. I might be able to give you some help."

There was nothing insincere in her voice or face, nothing I picked up as affected.

"My mother'll kill *me* if I do that."

"Could be what you need," Catherine said. "An outside assessment."

"Do you read a lot?"

"Tons, Kurt. I'm an intelligent reader."

"I've never seen you with a book."

"I read at home. Guess you didn't use that telescope of yours to look through my windows enough."

Alcohol damages thinking, to state nothing new, and I'll bet the amount I'd consumed with Catherine played its part in influencing my decision.

"You helped me with Ralph's body. This is my chance to help you out."

I didn't quite see the equivalence between moving a man's corpse to bury it and reading a manuscript for a critique, but I was delighted she'd acknowledged my assistance.

About fucking time! It seemed like an offer I could in good conscience accept, though the hairs that prickled along my spine should have been a warning I heeded.

"If she hears I let you read it…"

"Who's gonna tell her? I won't."

"You swear?"

"I take an oath. You want blood?"

"That's okay."

"I've never seen a man so scared of his mother."

"It's not fear" I said. "It's how unpleasant things can get listening to her bitch and grumble."

Catherine got up off the bed, pinching her cigarette out in my wineglass. She lifted her jacket and bent her arms into the sleeves.

"I'll start on it tomorrow. Have a copy for me?"

"Not printed."

"Flash drive?"

I did the transfer to a blank I had, then put the device in her hand. Placing it there, I felt as if I was giving her a bomb that could blow up my life.

Give it back. Can I have it back?

I wanted to say this, did not. I should have said this. And before I got another word out, Catherine had pussyfooted from my room and down the two flights of stairs.

At least my mother hadn't woken up.

Through my window, I watched Catherine drive away.

TWENTY-ONE

I hadn't dreamt of Charlotte in months. But that night I did. I throttled her neck with my hand and looked into her glassy eyes. I was lying on a bed and could feel her slack body beneath me. Then she twitched, as if having a spasm, and her stringy auburn hair fell over her face. If I could only bring my other hand up and push her hair aside to see her face again, but my hand remained down below, somewhere between our waists. I couldn't move it.

She was moaning or choking, coming from the sex or fading into a death rattle…

No shock to have a hangover in the morning, and with my headache and parched throat came the thought that I'd made a mistake. I couldn't doubt I had, remembering. To give Catherine a copy of the manuscript…what had I been thinking? Under the influence or not, why had I accepted her offer to read it? What was I hoping to accomplish? I'd never signed a confidentiality agreement with my mother, but she'd told me more than once not to breathe a word about the book to anyone until it was finished. Say nothing, let no one see it. Don't even give a peek to an agent or editor. She might kick me from the house if my action came to light, put me on the street in the dead of winter. Then what? No work, no home, little money. The downside of my mistake. The upside, though, it dawned on me, would mean I'd be released from the book. Done with the agonizing power game my mother and I had going. Was that the idea? To free myself? Damn twisted way of breaking loose. And as I'd told Catherine, I wanted to complete the book. No way around it: I'd invested too much of my time and energy not to see it through. I needed to have something to show for the effort, a fully rendered work. And also, if she fired me, would she bring in a new ghostwriter? Stupid worry, I know, but I didn't want anyone mucking up the pages I'd crafted.

Take your hands off my sentences, asshole. I sweat blood for that shit.

I considered breaking into Catherine's house to retrieve the zip drive. But unless she left it out somewhere, on a desk or table, I'd never find it, and even if I did, there was no guarantee she hadn't made copies off the drive already and stored the documents in her computer. I considered calling and asking her to bring it back right away, without copying files or printing pages, but I feared that asking for it back might embolden her somehow. If I showed too much eagerness to have it back, she'd know too well that she had leverage over me and I didn't know where that might lead. What were her intentions anyway? Now that my error was made, did she want to use her possession of the manuscript to get something out of me? I realized that I'd handed the book over to a total fucking stranger. What did I know about her anyhow? Still nothing about what she lived on, whether she worked, if she had a criminal past — none of that. And yet I'd up and handed over something she knew she could make me squirm with, if she threatened to tell my mother.

Give away leverage, gain nothing. Great job.

And I'm thirty-five years old, I thought, living like this. Sorry ass idiot.

As I got out of bed, head throbbing, and made my way toward the bathroom to grab myself a couple of aspirin, I decided I would sit tight to see what move she made. She might make none. Maybe she intended to read the manuscript to give me constructive advice. Maybe I should take her at her word. She'd read it, return it to me with notes, and my mother would never even know anything.

No harm done. A mistake without consequence. It happens.

My ass!

TWENTY-TWO

Or not my ass. I didn't want to be paranoid, did I? Or overly pessimistic? My mother didn't know that a woman had come to the house and she had no inkling a night later that when I left the house after dinner it was not to go drink alone at a bar or to try picking up women. Catherine had called, and she asked me to meet her again at the Fieldhouse Tavern. Did I have much choice? I said okay. I was past my hangover from the morning and ready to resume drinking with her. But I wouldn't let myself get wasted. Not tonight. I needed a clear head, and self-control was the key. She'd given no tip-off about what she had on her mind.

We got our drinks and took our booth. Catherine's hair was done in a ponytail and she had on subtle red lipstick. She didn't hand the zip drive back or mention when she might. But she said she'd spent all day reading the book and plied me with questions about it, wanting to know how I'd come to write it. Her interest in it seemed real, and as we talked, a curious thought coalesced: she was reading it to learn more about me. Through reading my writing, through reading my telling of my mother's story, she thought she might get insight into her watcher. Something in the ether had reversed itself, sparking the observed to become the observer and me the observer to become the observed. I felt myself liking her attention, and under her spotlight, I told her about the years of writing, the pieces accepted and rejected, the novels started and abandoned. I didn't have to tell her about the *New Yorker* piece; she'd found that when she Googled my name.

"Some story about your father."

"It is," I said.

"Is the woman who did it still in jail?"

"Oh yeah. She ain't getting out anytime soon."

Catherine called the memoir readable, its style direct. And my mother's youth, the years spent on three continents, in Paris, Morocco, New York, was a subject worthy of a book. What threw her, though, she said, were the sex scenes in it, the pages of erotic detail. There was something distasteful about these parts, unsavory, a grown man living with his mother and chronicling her teenage sexual adventures.

"I still have her college years to write," I said. "There's more."

"More. And that's no big deal for you?"

"They're the hardest parts. I've got to get into the head of a girl discovering orgasms."

"But it's not any girl. It's your mother."

"That makes it tougher. I agree."

"Tougher?" Catherine said. "Just tougher? It's kind of sick, Kurt."

"You reading the book to psychoanalyze me?"

"You've been stalking me, Kurt. Can you blame me if I wanna know what's in your head?"

Honesty was fair, honesty was fine, and since she was pursuing it, I decided to also. Who was she, I said, to lay into me when she had kinks of her own? Damn, man, did she have issues: how would she describe her visits to June Hazzard's grave? Until recently, when she stopped, she'd gone three or four times a week — no variation. That didn't reek of something unwholesome? Her reaction to the unexpected, Ralph Soames' trespass, had been off the charts, and I didn't know what to say about the knife she'd drawn in the tomb. Whenever I alluded to that evening, she led the discussion somewhere else. For crying out loud, she'd acted as if she thought I'd popped into her life for the express purpose of ending it. She'd spoken like June Hazzard was alive and I her agent of death.

"I had my reasons for thinking that."

"I'm waiting to hear them," I said. "Is she dead or not? And can you tell me why you told the cops Ralph Soames is missing?"

"I didn't tell them he's missing. I told them he's dead."

"Jesus. When?"

"The morning after it happened."

"Why?"

"Because he was," Catherine said.

She'd driven to the station and told them she killed a man, but when the cops had gone to investigate, they found blood without a body.

"When I heard that," Catherine said, squinting one eye, voice on the loud side. "When I heard that his body wasn't there, I freaked. What could I think but he hadn't died? But he never turned up anywhere and his car was gone and I was frantic till you came knocking with your note. It did explain what happened to Ralph."

And her information addressed the question that had been bothering me for days — why the police had gotten on a "missing person's case" so speedily.

"You told them the killing was intentional?" I said.

"I called it an accident," Catherine answered, voice under control again. "Which it was. I told them I pushed him and he hit his head."

"But have you spoken to the cops since?"

"Twice. They questioned me. Now they don't know what happened to him or whether I even told the truth. They know something happened because of the blood they have but—"

"This is since we met?"

"Obviously. They don't have a body but I must be a suspect or whatever. Maybe they think I'm crazy."

"But if this is since we met—"

"Getting the picture?" Catherine said, smiling as if she'd make a joke. "I've been actively shielding you. Never mentioned you."

"Why would you do that?"

"You went above and beyond for me. That counts for something."

"Does it? Don't know if I can believe that."

"You did."

"Before you said I fucked you up. That you can't go back to the tomb."

"That, too. But I respect what you did for me."

"And you're glad Soames is gone? I thought you liked him."

"I didn't dislike him," Catherine said. "He passed the time, provided certain things."

Like what? I remembered what Soames had said to me suggesting he'd never had sex with her, but it didn't sound like she missed the guy even on a friendship level.

"So what do you think the cops think?" I said.

"What can they think? That I killed him and hid the body myself? Then reported it? Why? Or that I'm telling the truth and he suffered a head injury, maybe amnesia, and he's gone off somewhere? With the car gone, it looks like he could've driven off after coming to, in some sort of state."

"What a mess."

"Not entirely. If I hold tight, I'm safe. So are you. The cops come back to speak to you again?"

"Not so far. But they spoke to my mother. I mention that?"

"Don't think so."

"They did. Before they spoke to me."

"Does she know about this?" Catherine asked.

"She has ideas because I was gone from the house so long. That night, the next day."

"That's not good."

"She hasn't said any of that to them. For her, if I just keep working on the book, she doesn't care."

"Another reason to stick with it then," Catherine said. "Is that it?"

"Don't want to tick her off, no."

"She'd rat you out to the cops? Your own mother?"

"If I bailed on the book, she might."

"Guess you should keep doing it then."

"Don't quit, you're saying now. Don't leave."

"You could kill her."

"Thought runs through my mind every day," I said. "I told you that."

"So you did. Listen. Just don't crumble, whatever you decide, and don't give anything away to the cops. You do that and we should be in the clear."

We? Had Catherine said *we?* She saw us as being in this together then, conspirators, and I began to relax somewhat. When she'd gone to the police after I told her I'd buried Soames' body, she might've been able to help herself at my expense. She'd been involved in an accident (she'd have to make the cops believe that, of course); my actions had been deliberate. I was more liable under the law. But she hadn't followed up with the cops, and now the knowledge she had and withheld from them made her as culpable as I was. By choice, she'd aligned herself with me. My thoughts of her using the book against me might've been panic and nothing else.

"To secrecy," I said, hoisting my glass of rum and Coke.

"Secrecy," Catherine said. "I'll drink to that."

She clinked her glass against mine and we drank. Finished what we had. Then she rose and went to the bar to order us a second round.

"Catherine?" I said, after she'd returned.

"Yeah."

"I have to get something straight if I can."

"Go ahead."

"Here now as we speak, as we drink, you have no interest in going to jail?"

"None."

"But before you did, when you called the police."

"I thought it's what she wanted," Catherine said. "Punishment for me."

"Wanted? A dead person?"

"I thought we just toasted to privacy."

"To secrecy," I said. "From the cops."

"Ah, yes. I'm talking to a stalker, not exactly a guy who respects privacy."

"Is June dead or not?"

"She's dead, Kurt. She's in the tomb."

So her sickness had to do with superstition, a believe in ghosts or some such thing, and I would have to cut through that nonsense if I was going to get anywhere with her.

"I think I'm starting to get it," I said. "To understand."

"Don't condescend to me, Kurt. Momma's boy."

"I'm not. I'm just saying..." But I wanted to think, to be alone. After this talk, I needed that. I asked Catherine if we could call it a night and she voiced no opposition, leaving the booth without saying goodbye.

Fuck you, too, I thought, but I knew I wasn't done with her. I knew I was going to make her see that I was more important than any dead person. Tell my mother about the book? Go ahead. Won't make a difference. I'm going to arrange something for you, myself, and June. That's the threesome that counts here.

TWENTY-THREE

I'm not a violent person. I didn't get into fights at school and I don't remember scuffling with anyone as an adult. What transpired with Charlotte began as consensual activity, then degenerated from there. And that activity wasn't violent in the true sense; it involved the use of paraphernalia. None of which is what killed her; the drugs did that. But our time together did leave me with handcuffs. A few sets. I didn't have to buy any for what I had planned. Overpowering Catherine would be the hard part, and my Internet research suggested that chloroform was more a staple of crime fiction than an option that would work in real life. Too much struggle to hold a rag over someone's mouth; people don't pass out in seconds like they show in the movies. But how else to do it? I didn't own a gun and I had no wish to put a knife to her throat. The brutality of holding a blade against her neck revolted me, and one slip by either of us could lead to bloodshed. In the end, I went with the best of all the bad options, a stun gun, ordered from a website. The gag would be a strip of bed sheet.

Here's where I tried to show sensitivity — as much as I could within my framework. The sheet used for the gag was silk, top quality, and I'd bought it special for the occasion. I hoped to convey to Catherine that I wanted her to feel well-treated while she had the gag in her mouth.

She'd be infuriated once she recovered from the voltage blast. I got that. But I needed her to understand that despite the restraints, despite the brief trip I would force her on, I meant her no harm.

I parked in her driveway, behind her car. Turned off my headlights. Felt for the stun gun on the passenger seat, the knapsack with the cuffs and gag. The question here was would she answer when I phoned. If she didn't, I'd have to approach some other way. I didn't want to cut a window to invade her house, risk the panic and violence that might come with that.

She took the call after three rings.

"What, Kurt?"

"Glad you're still up."

"I don't sleep much. What do you want?"

"We have to talk."

"Your questions never end, do they?"

"This isn't about June Hazzard."

"What then?"

"Can we talk? I'm right outside."

"This can't wait till morning?"

"The cops came over again today and I don't like what my mother told them."

"What did she say?"

"Do we have to talk about it like this? Can I come in?"

"You can't come in, Kurt."

"How about at the bar? I'm freezing here."

A long sigh.

"I was just arguing with her. She's angry at me because she found out about you and—"

"You need to get a grip on your shit, Kurt. She's *your* mother."

"But this involves us both."

"Oh my God! The terror of Mom! Wait there."

When she opened the door, I applied the taser to her left shoulder. I held it there for a count of five. Ugly and crude, but she dropped as expected, convulsing on the carpet in her black down jacket.

In my driveway, I lifted Catherine out of my car. I'd wrapped her in a quilted blanket for warmth, but it wasn't as cold as I'd suggested while standing on her stoop. The polar snap had passed and the air smelled of pinewood, a pre-spring scent blowing over from the hills. There was no moon, but the blue-black sky had no clouds either. I'd never seen a moonless night so clear, and as I walked past the gravestones with Catherine slung across my shoulder, I thought of how exposed I was to view. When I'd left the house earlier, my mother was reading in bed; by now, she should be out. But what if in her sleep, uncanny woman, she'd heard me pull up in the driveway, kill the engine, and not enter the house. She might come outside to see whether everything was all right. She'd think I'd come home drunk again and fallen on my face in the yard. Would she interfere with me if she saw me walking in the graveyard with a body? Or call the cops? She'd have to, I thought, one or the other.

Inside the tomb, in the back chamber, I sat Catherine down. Cuffed at her wrists and ankles, she didn't fight me, and I placed her back against a tomb wall. I arranged her facing June Hazzard's coffin, and while she watched, I took out my lighter. I lit the candles on the white sarcophagus. All six were short, burnt down, but they would last awhile.

"I want to show you something," I said. "Eyes here."

If Catherine's face had ever been as red as her hair, this was the time.

I busied myself with the candles, lifting them one at a time off the coffin. All six stood in long brass holders, and the flames leaned and danced as I set each one on the floor. I scrooched down, knees together, and put my thumb into a hole in the floor's concrete. A small hole, thumb-diameter size. I hadn't noticed it till my visit the other day to the tomb, when I'd taken the time, seized by a thought, to canvass every foot of that chamber.

My thumb touched a metal spring, pushed. The coffin's lid started to move, sliding back from one end. I saw the rollers, gears, and grooves in the lid, apparatus befitting a medieval device, and a human face was revealed. When the lid clunked to a stop three quarters of the way down the coffin, I turned back around toward Catherine.

"Did you design this? It's so Gothic, it's almost quaint."

The embalming was wondrous. The long blonde hair had the sheen of a living woman's hair. But the eyes, which were open, these grabbed me the most; June Hazzard's eyes were greyish-blue lasers, bedazzling eyes observing me.

Or so it appeared. I moved in a circle around the coffin, confirming something. Sure enough, the eyes never left my face, though they did not move. How could they? The woman was dead. Somehow the body's eyes contained the Mona Lisa effect, following me inside the chamber. I couldn't account for the effect, but I felt that it worked in

Graveyard Love

my favor. The persistent attention from those eyes fed into what I intended to do.

Under the blue quilt, Catherine kicked her legs. She made snuffling noises through her gag. Undeterred, I knelt beside her, and I put my right hand around her neck while weaving my left through her hair. The red strands were tied in a ponytail.

"Hold still," I said. "I don't want to hurt you."

Maybe it was my tone, or that she accepted her helplessness, but she stopped kicking. She became quiet. Her eyes never left mine and I knew she was frightened because she was breathing fast. I considered taking out the gag but thought she might scream. And if she did that loud enough for my mother to hear? I doubted a scream would carry as far as the house, but at this time of night, with the quiet, I couldn't risk it.

Rising, I stared at June. In her tight white feather-frilled dress, she had a sublime decolletage. She was narrow-waisted and curvy, and her skin had the smooth appearance of a pearl. Alive she must've been seductive, I thought, quite the enchantress, and the sight of her unfaded beauty along with Catherine lying there close got me going. Arousal hit, the erection sudden. I bent down by Catherine again, took her arm, brushed my lips against her cheek. I was careful to keep my tongue in my mouth, but she cringed at my kiss.

"Is it really that bad? It's necessary."

I lifted her to her feet and the quilt fell to the floor. I let her stand against the tomb wall, her cuffed wrists at her waist. Pornographic images scrolled through my mind, and I felt the temptation to remove her jacket, sweatshirt, and jeans. Strip her naked, go all the way. How could I not imagine that? For so damn long, I'd been thinking about doing what I pleased to Catherine, with or without her consent.

Mind on the goal. This is for her therapy. Her mental health. Don't let your dick rule you.

"We need June watching us," I said.

I caressed Catherine and allowed my hands to roam. Upper body, lower body, breasts, pelvis. I immersed myself in my healing task, then noticed that Catherine, face pale, had closed her eyes.

"Look at June. Right at her. You see her watching this?"

I wasn't lying. In everything I did to Catherine, June's eyes seemed to be on us.

TWENTY-FOUR

I removed the gag when I got back inside her house. I warned her that if she started yelling, the gag would go right back in. The handcuffs remained, but I laid her on her living room sofa, head braced by a cushion. I knew it was time to reveal myself and tell her why I'd fondled her in front of June. But first, since I was there, I decided to explore her house and see what I could learn about her that way. Not the best etiquette, understood, but curiosity got the best of me.

A dining room, kitchen, living room, bathroom, and bedroom. That's what Catherine had. She had a basement but no garage, and all the rooms except the bathroom, which had an enormous old-time tub with gold-plated spigots for the hot and cold water, were modest in size. She had no photos of June Hazzard anywhere, which surprised me, and her books, neat in a living room bookcase, tended toward the esoteric. Volumes on the tarot deck, the history of spiritualism, ghosts. Titles with the words "Death," "Soul," and "Mind" in them. I can't claim I was shocked, though the bird-watching books threw me for a loop. The kitchen had a full array of cooking implements, and a multi-geared bike near the front door told me what she did for fitness. Besides that, in her bedroom, she owned a laptop and a flat screen TV, but nothing clued me in to what she did for money or whether she had a profession.

"Bird-watching, huh?"

I was back in the living room, seated in a wing chair across from the sofa.

"You done with your inspection?"

"So you understand the impulse to watch."

"You drawing a comparison between bird-watching and what you do?"

"There are similarities."

"How's this going to end?" Catherine said. "You gonna fuck me finally? Kill me? Kill me then fuck me?"

"I can see how you might think that."

"You can? Wow! Impressive. I'll take it the fun you had before was your foreplay."

"If you'd let me explain."

"Now you sound like a guilty husband, Kurt."

"You don't seem scared."

"I'm just tired. Tired of men."

"And now *you* sound like my mother. Don't think she's been with a guy since my father."

"You should know. Writing the story of her life and all."

Catherine rolled onto her side, legs drawn up, and faced the sofa's back rest. I was looking at her hair against the black of her jacket, the shape of her ass in her jeans. Her turn away from me seemed to be saying the talk was over, that I should do something physical or leave, but I couldn't abide by either choice.

"Let me tell you what this is about," I said.

"Please do," Catherine said. "I'm on pins and needles."

"So you are listening."

"Do I have a choice?"

"You know I like horror movies, right? You saw my collection when you came over."

"So?" She corkscrewed herself, staring at me over her shoulder. "You want to recreate something from a movie?"

"No. Nothing like that. But a horror movie helped me see what's going on."

"Going on with what?"

"With you," I said. "I was watching it again the other night and had a light bulb moment."

"You need help, Kurt. You have to see that. Can't we just end this and look into that? I'll do my best to help you find someone."

"I'm trying to help *you* here. Let's stay on point."

"Have you ever been?"

"Been what?"

"To a psychiatrist."

"Don't you want to know which movie?" I said. "The one that helped me see what's going on?"

She rolled back over to face me, downcast.

"Tell me."

"*Cat People*."

"Don't know it."

"There's two. But I'm talking about the original, from 1943."

Props to Val Lewton and Dewitt Bodeen, who wrote the movie, and also to director Jacques Tourneur. Their low budget classic is so psychologically astute. Set in New York, *Cat People* tells the story of a Serbian-born woman named Irena. She's young and pretty, but haunted by a fear she descends from a race of cursed cavewomen. These women, whenever they become sexually aroused, turn into destructive panthers, she believes. "Kiss me and I'll claw you to death," read the ads, but the movie itself is low-key. It never becomes sensationalistic. It's a shadowy, suggestive film that deals more with the fear of sex than with a monster. It is also, for my money, the best curse-themed story in cinema, and the recent night I'd watched it again, I couldn't help but see the traits shared by Irena and Catherine Embers.

Much about Catherine could be explained based on one premise. If she was superstitious, truly so, if Catherine believed herself cursed, her maddening actions did have a logic. It all started with June Hazzard. She was dead, and in all probability, she was Catherine's former lover. But supposing before she died (however she died), June had said or done something that made Catherine think she would be punished if she ever took another lover. What if that had happened? It meant that Catherine had flouted the curse when she hooked up with Ralph Soames, and lo and behold, the man soon lost his life. There was proof of June's awesome power. Take a lover, Catherine, and bad things will come your way. Then I had appeared at her house, my timing perfect, and Catherine saw me as the curse's tool, the agent of June's retribution. Hence her giving me the knife in the vault, hence her belief I'd kill her. And when I'd refused, voicing my horror, she broke down in tears and understood: I wasn't there to fulfill the curse and punish her for taking a post-June lover.

Delusion? Maybe. Delusion in Catherine. But from that premise of a curse, a curse she felt June had placed on her, everything else followed. My thesis accounted for Catherine's vagaries and why she used the present tense when referring to June Hazzard. For her, June was alive. She lived on through her curse. And though Catherine knew in her head that I was no agent of any curse, she still half-believed in the curse's efficacy and couldn't bring herself to flout it again by letting us go to bed. She was all ambivalence now about sex and whether or not we could have a relationship.

"A relationship?" Catherine said, when I stopped talking. "You call what we have a relationship?"

"It could be. If it wasn't for June as an influence."

I stood and flexed my arms, keyed up from the cracking of the mystery.

"Am I right more or less? About the curse."

"You're a regular Sherlock Holmes."

"I knew it," I said. "Do you want to see the movie? I can bring it over and we'll watch it together."

"I'll get the popcorn," Catherine said.

"I'm serious, Catherine. You're like Irena and I'm like the boyfriend in the film, trying to tell her there's no curse."

"But there was a curse in the end, you said."

"It's a horror movie, Catherine. There has to be something."

"And I don't turn into a panther when I get turned on."

"Not that part," I said. "The psychological part. You got close to Soames and thought he died for it."

"He died because I pushed him. End of story."

"And you understand that?"

"I do now," Catherine said. She'd wriggled into a sitting position, feet to the floor. "So you didn't have to feel me up like you wanted to prove something to June. Who's the one who believes she's a presence? You or me?"

"Point taken. But I wanted to make sure."

"Sure of what?"

"That you know she has no sway over you. You can move forward with your life."

"You know the psychological jargon, I'll give you that."

"Say what you want. I'm trying to help you work through your issues, Catherine."

"You stun-gun me, handcuff me, do everything but rape me. You call that 'working through'?"

I sat in the wing chair again, on its front edge, determined to keep plugging. Nobody said doing therapy's easy, and I can't make any claims to being trained in it. But I felt I could get her to warm toward me if I made her see my motives were good. My objective was to help her face her baggage, and my unorthodox methods served that objective.

"Consider the handcuffs a restraint and me your doctor."

I was trying to add levity, lighten the talk.

"I won't and you aren't."

"I've done a lot for you, Catherine."

"Kurt." She shut her eyes again, then looked straight at me. "I thank you for burying Ralph. I really do. From the bottom of my heart, thanks."

"You're welcome."

"It was a gutsy thing to do and I know it means you care."

"I've been hoping to hear you say that."

"Fantastic. But I also wish there was a curse. I sincerely do. I'd fuck you in a second, this instant, if I thought you were going to die afterwards. It'd be the easiest way to get rid of you."

TWENTY-FIVE

I should've slapped her for that, but didn't. How could I? I don't hit women, never have. Charlotte knew how to test my patience and during writing sessions there'd been times that I was tempted to whack my mother, but when my temper flared and I felt I might get violent, I'd close my eyes, take a breath, and count to five. Or count to ten. Depending on how long the anger stayed. The eyes/breath/counting technique is what I used now, while Catherine watched me, and when I opened my eyes and continued breathing (fifteen seconds), I jumped up from the chair and bowed like a Prussian soldier. I gave her a salute and made for the door, leaving her manacled on the couch.

"Hey."

I could hear her surprise, and fear.

"Kurt?"

But why answer? I didn't know what to say to her. Therapy takes time and practice. Did I have either? Was it worth grinding away with her? How could I have been optimistic? To break down her defenses and make her see why she should like me, that I had nothing but love for her, would be an ordeal. And let's face it. Zapping her with the taser, binding her wrists and ankles, and pawing her in the tomb had not helped my cause. My *Cat People* theory, which I thought sound, dead on, had elicited scorn.

Fighting back tears (I'm not joking), I drove home.

In the kitchen, as quietly as I could, I put a pan on the stove and boiled some water. I sprinkled instant oatmeal into a bowl. Maple and brown sugar, my favorite variety. Soft pink light was seeping through the window, and as I ate, I stared across the street, over at the graveyard. Everything had begun there. I'd seen Catherine during an evening walk, and in short order, numbskull of numbskulls, allowed myself to become obsessed. What does Freud call it? The compulsion to repeat? Out of one harmful relationship — with Charlotte, and lucky to survive that — and into another. But who was I trying to kid? I had no relationship with Catherine. Tonight she'd drilled that reality home. Beyond her gratitude for my help, and reluctant gratitude at that, she felt nothing for me. Nothing except annoyance and contempt. And had these grown into outright hostility? After tonight, they might have. But it was too late to apologize. Should I just leave her there? How long does it take for a person to starve to death? Weeks, I calculated, two or three, and in that time she might get a visitor. A friend, if she had any, or a package delivery. The mailman. I hadn't put the gag back in her mouth so all she had to do was keep on yelling till someone heard her. She might be screaming right now. *Blunder after blunder*, I told myself, *there's nothing with her I've done that's smart*, and while I was thinking that I could try to escape somewhere, drive to the airport, buy a ticket and go — who knows? — to South America, my mother came into the kitchen, early in her rising as always. She was the last person I wanted to see.

"Morning, ma."

"You're up early."

"It happens."

"Bad dreams?"

"I had a few thoughts on where we should go with the next chapter."

"Is that what woke you?"

"I think so," I said.

"You look like hell."

"I do?"

"Like you never went to sleep."

Can you fool your own mother? Fuck. She knew me too well. I must've had bags under my eyes and the dry flakiness that sprouts on my face when I don't get enough sleep. There was no use arguing with her.

In her long blue robe my mother went about her morning ritual. She measured coffee into the filter, poured in the water, turned on the machine, took her mug from the cabinet and put it on the counter, waited. Two teaspoons of sugar in the mug, cigarette lit. Then she was drinking her black coffee between voluminous puffs on the cigarette, and she didn't join me at the table but kept her weight on the sink counter, standing against it. The eyes on me must have been the eyes cross-examined witnesses saw back in her lawyer days.

"I'm seeing the signs again, Kurt."

"What signs?"

"The ones that were there when you went through everything with Charlotte."

"What are you talking about?"

"The manic behavior. Staying out all night. The secretive trips."

"I'm not manic," I said. "And what would you know about how I was then? I was in the city."

"You came up here to stay for a month, remember?"

"Did I?"

"For breathing room from her, you said."

"Sounds crazy now," I said. "Since I'm living with a person who doesn't give any breathing room."

"You're dodging the issue, Kurt. And I'm not blind. I can see the stress in your face."

"Can I finish my oatmeal in peace?"

"Eat. I'm not stopping you. But you know when it started? The signs, the strain?"

"When I was dumb enough to agree to work on your book?"

"After the night you went to the city," my mother said.

"What night I went to the city?"

"You know the night I mean," she said.

"That's silly."

"Not so silly the cops didn't come here asking questions."

"That's their job," I said. "They were investigating something."

"Save it," my mother said. "Whatever you told the cops seems to have convinced them. But there's something going on, I know it. Should I be getting you a lawyer?"

"Mom!"

"Should I?"

"No," I said. "Now can I get some rest?"

"You *are* sleepy then?"

"I was at a woman's house," I said. "Okay? You want details?"

"Like I said, it's the Charlotte situation all over again."

I couldn't take the circularity of her discourse, that attorney ability to direct a conversation toward a specified end.

Point to my mother for bringing the talk back where she wanted it to go.

"Do you want to get any writing done today, ma?"

"That depends on you."

"If you let me get some shut-eye. Two, three hours and I'll be ready to go."

"Whatever you say. It's not like your mind's been on it recently."

"What makes you say that?"

"The quality of the writing. It's fallen off."

Upstairs, I brushed my teeth and changed into pajamas. I pulled the blankets over my head, my position fetal. The position symbolic of the time before you make a mess of things, when you know nothing but have no worries either. What most irked me was that I still knew zip about Catherine. Despite my heated interaction with her, what did I know? Did she have a job? What was the source of her income? Did she own or rent her house? I knew she and June had been lovers, but specifics about their relationship, how they'd met, what they'd done together, were unknown to me. Googling the name June Hazzard had brought no hits, and Catherine had never revealed anything. I didn't even know what June looked like when she was alive. *Inept as an investigator*, I thought, toying with the idea of getting up and returning to Catherine's. If she hadn't freed herself yet, I could gag her again and comb through every inch of her house. Photos, bills, diaries, her phone, the computer — there had to be tidbits about her I'd learn through a study of her possessions. I should have done that before at her place instead of reading the titles of her books and seeing what she had in her kitchen.

Could one reset the clock? Could I rewind time to the moment before I'd seen Catherine? On a second go-round, I'd take a different tack and ignore her visits to the graveyard. I'd rise above myself and master my compulsion. I wouldn't get infatuated. The energy and time I'd wasted on my Catherine pursuits! Without those, I could've finished the memoir already and started work on my own book.

For distraction, to get away from my thoughts, I needed music. I retrieved my phone from the pants on my desk chair, plucked the headphones up from my bedside table. What was I in the mood for? Something serene, graceful: I scrolled through the menu in my phone and alighted on Gabriel Faure, his *Requiem*.

As the piece began, I lay down and closed my eyes. For a millisecond, I considered driving back to Catherine's house to free her from the handcuffs. If she hadn't started yelling, or called anyone, there might yet be time for that. I could free her and apologize. Ask her forgiveness. But that would mean getting up again and going downstairs and past my mother, and I didn't feel I had the energy. Any way I could move the handcuff keys by telekinesis? From my pants to Catherine's hands? No, not on this planet, but it was relaxation time, mental escape time, and I let the *Requiem* waft me away. I wheeled, I ascended, I had a vision of myself talking with Catherine, smiling at her while she smiled at me, and I was stroking her long red hair.

I don't know when, but I must have fallen asleep. Because then, next thing I knew, my name was being called.

"Kurt. Kurt."

Graveyard Love

I opened my eyes, trying to see in the sunlight. My lips and cheeks felt wet and I had to remove the headphones from my ears.

"What is it, ma?"

"Get dressed and come downstairs."

"Why? I need to sleep."

"Someone's here to see you."

"Who? The police?"

"No," my mother said. "Are you expecting the police?"

"Who's here?"

"A woman I think you know. Her name's Catherine Embers."

TWENTY-SIX

She looked at home sitting at our kitchen table. She looked, how shall I say, fucking comfortable. A cup of tea, the sugar bowl, a spoon, and a white paper napkin had been laid out for her. No handcuffs anywhere on her body, and she had on the jeans and black down jacket she'd been wearing before.

"I waited for you to come back," she said. "But you didn't."

From her to my mother I kept glancing back and forth, dizzy.

"She's promised not to press charges," my mother said.

Cigarette going, she'd sat at the table, too; I was the only person standing. My mother's coffee cup was quarter full.

"I'm not...I'm not getting this," I said.

"I called," Catherine said. "What's so complicated?"

"I didn't hear my phone ring."

"Called your house," she said. "Your number's listed."

That she'd dragged or rolled herself over to her phone I understood, but why on earth would she contact my mother?

"You never know with mothers and their sons," she said, "but I had a feeling she wouldn't approve. You said she was a lawyer. Handcuffing women? Didn't think she'd like that."

"Where are the cuffs?"

"Kurt." My mother speaking. "Think about what you did."

"Where are the goddamn cuffs?" I asked.

"I took them off," my mother answered. "They're at Catherine's house."

"But the keys were in my pants."

"And your pants were on your chair. First place to look for keys."

"You don't even ask? You came tiptoeing into my room like a thief."

"Kurt, you handcuffed a woman against her will. You left her in that state. Do you know how lucky you are that she's not pressing charges?"

Luck has nothing to do with it, I thought, and wondered what countermove Catherine had planned. She had something in mind: why else had she called my mother? There were other ways she could have gotten free. And how much had she told my mother about everything involving us two?

The incongruity of the situation, to be in a room with my two nemeses, made the air seem thin. I felt as if I was breathing through a straw. Could I get away by dissolving through the floor and arising from the earth someplace else? I should've put Catherine down earlier, when I had her defenseless, but now that chance was gone. Or was it? Having them both so close meant I could do them both in a jiffy. Grab the cutting knife from the set in the rack on the counter. Charge with it. Don't stab. Slit their throats. But what were the odds I'd avoid arrest? Soames had disappeared and he was tied to Catherine who'd been seen in public with me, a guy who lived with his mother. If three of four people connected in a case vanished, I'd be suspect number one by default. I'd be handing the cops an arrest.

"Can I borrow him for awhile?" Catherine said.

"If you promise to bring him back," my mother said, winking.

"I will."

"Be my guest."

Who were they talking about? Did I get a say?

"I'm not going with you," I said. "Why would I?"

Catherine stood. "Let's go for a drive, Kurt."

"Are you deaf? I'm not going."

"Scared of me now?"

"I'm not scared. We're done, that's all."

"Kurt." My mother again. "Go with her. After what you did, it's amazing she wants to be anywhere near you."

"Care to let me know why we're going for a drive?"

"For a coffee," Catherine said. "For old time's sake."

That sounded like bullshit, but I dropped my resistance. Whatever would happen would happen. And anything was better than being in a room with them both.

We drove through the brightness of a sunny morning, on winding roads. We passed farm silos and barns, level cornfields, a pond or two. Spring was coming, green buds and shoots, and I powered my window down a bit. Catherine talked nonstop, though she didn't look at me. I took it that she wanted me to listen without interrupting, so that's what I did. To boil it down: she told me that she was moving away and never wanted to hear from me again. We wouldn't meet, we wouldn't talk by phone, we wouldn't stay in touch through email. Nada. It had to be a definitive break. The catch was that in order to move she needed a helping hand from me. She had something she wished she could do by herself, but the physical part of the job in question made doing it alone impossible. And while movers would do the lifting in her house, no one except me could help with the other thing she needed to transport.

"It's June," she said. "So she can come with me."

"June? You mean her body?"

"June."

"You're going to dig her up."

"She's not buried, Kurt. You know that. We take her out, put her in another coffin, something lighter, and you can help me get it into a truck. Then it's goodbye forever. I don't have to see you again."

"What if I said I'll leave you alone? Come see her body whenever you want?"

"You ruined the place for me, Kurt. I told you that. You and Ralph Soames."

"It's just a tomb."

"Not to me," she said. "But you don't get that."

"I defiled your sacred place, you're saying?"

"You ruined it, ass-face. Isn't that enough?"

"You can't blame me for wondering what you were doing in there. I still don't know."

"What's the matter with men?" Catherine said. "You can't leave a woman a space to be private. You have to piss on everything?"

"I just wanted you to like me," I said.

"You're the one who should move away," she said. "But you won't. You're there with mommy, and she and you got your own tango going. Good luck with that."

"Did the cops say you could leave town?"

"They never said I couldn't."

I wished I knew where the cops were with Ralph Soames' disappearance, but wherever their investigation was, they hadn't found enough to charge Catherine with anything. Or me, if I was on their radar. Whatever they had, it couldn't be much, and there'd been nothing about Soames for weeks in the local paper.

"Let's cut to it, Kurt. You gonna help? You do, we're done, goodbye. You don't, I go back to your mother. It'd make her day to hear about how you gave me her book to read."

Catherine shot a look at me, then returned her attention to driving.

"I didn't mention it earlier," she said. "But she's mad enough at you as it is. Imagine if she hears about that?"

"You didn't show it to anyone, did you?"

"Not yet," Catherine said. "I could leak it on the Internet, though. That'll please her."

"What did you two talk about?"

"How I got handcuffed. I picked up a vibe from her that…your history with women's a not great one."

"What did she say?"

"Enough. Why don't you get help, Kurt?"

"You're the one who needs help," I said. "You're taking a dead woman with you when you move."

"Is it yes or no? I'm not going to wait all day for an answer."

I felt depleted sitting there, going through this talk with her, and had no more desire to argue. Why cling? I'd failed with Catherine. Once she left, I'd try to forget her.

"I'll help," I said. "To be honest, I'll be glad when you're gone."

"Then it's win-win."

"Fuck, I tried. You have a heart of ice."

"Poor Kurt."

I could hear her sarcasm.

"Poor guy."

She said she'd ring when she needed me, and drove me home.

TWENTY-SEVEN

I walked inside and up to my room. I knew my mother would follow fast so I didn't bother to lock the door. She'd only pound and pound till I opened it. I lay flat, shoes off, hands behind my head, and right on cue my mother entered, a white-crested stork in a black and white sweat suit.

"You want to talk about it?"

"No," I answered.

"What'd she say?"

"None of your business."

"Worst case? It's a kidnapping charge."

"I didn't kidnap her," I said.

"You confined her against her will."

"You heard her, mom. She's not going to the police."

"So you've dodged another bullet."

"Another?"

"Like with Charlotte."

"Can I please please please have some time for myself?"

"I'll give you that, Kurt. Gladly. But first you have to promise one thing."

"Which is?"

"Swear you'll check yourself in for treatment."

"No outpatient care? Therapy once or twice a week?"

"It's not a joke."

"I'm not laughing," I said.

"One day you won't be so lucky, and the woman you're with'll have your hide."

"Duly registered. Now will you please leave me alone?"

"Not until you say you'll do it. Consider it a rest. I'll pay."

"And the book?"

"We'll put it on hold. Or you'll work on it there. You should be allowed a laptop."

Seemed like during my drive with Catherine, she had mapped my confinement out. I was to go away, see doctors, talk and talk and talk about myself. Delve into the issue of my recurring behaviors with women. How I have an obsessive streak, and stalk. How I'm not above locking a woman up to try to win her affection. Why I might be like this. How the murder of my father had impacted my psyche or what my toilet training had been like. I couldn't envisage a bigger waste of time, and to compound the suggestion's effrontery, there was its injustice. If I did have an obsessive nature, a controlling side, where might these have come from? Mother, take a look at yourself in the fucking mirror. Would you call yourself a laid-back person? Is your attitude toward your book casual? No monomania there — none. Thanks for the genes, mom.

"Tell you what I'll do," I said. "I'll go in if you go also."

"Don't be silly."

"I'm not. We'll go together, shared therapy."

"I need a smoke," my mother said.

"And I need a drink. But yeah, I'm the one with the compulsions, you're not."

"I'd rather it be voluntary, Kurt."

"Are you threatening me? You can't have me committed."

"I'd prefer not to try," she said. "But I want you to get the help you need."

Second time in an hour someone had told me I need help, and each time the person telling me was a veritable nut themselves.

"Everyone loves to point," I said. "Fuck this."

I tied my shoes, combed my hair, zippered my coat. But my mother hadn't moved from the doorway.

"Excuse me."

"Where you going?"

"Out."

"Where?" my mother asked.

"Are you going to move or do I have to push you?"

"It'd better not be back to her," she said, stepping aside, letting me pass. "Please don't go back there. I'll call the police."

I stopped as if roped, face tingling. Everything tingled. Throughout my body, I felt a palpitating warmth.

"Madame." I took her frown for bona fide concern. "I merely want to escape the sound of your voice. Please allow me this freedom, or I won't be held accountable for my actions."

I did my Prussian soldier bow and fled.

"Don't go back there," my mother yelled. "It's trouble if you do."

At the Fieldhouse Tavern, the Corona with tequila shots did nothing to cool me down. I drank and got hotter, started to sweat. The moisture bunched underneath my arms and beaded my hairline. My shirt was sticking to my back. Acid bubbled up from my stomach and into my chest, and the more I drank, the drier my throat became. I could barely swallow. Something in me was off and I could feel my temples swelling, expanding outward from my head. I touched them to check their size, but they hadn't budged. My head retained its usual dimensions. The pressure was within, from my thoughts, and I wondered whether I should do something to alleviate it, take my mind off my setbacks. I could drive to Kingston, or the City, and buy myself a prostitute. I could spend the night fucking, drinking, slapping. How much extra for the slapping? It would have to be someone with red hair and I'd say I wanted to call her Catherine. Obvious, but so what? She wouldn't know the history behind the name. The pros act as surrogates all the time, and if I kept the slapping under control, or did no slapping, the night would be routine for her.

"You okay, Kurt?"

Tony doing his job, observing me from across the bar, watching his clientele's gestures and mutterings.

"I'm okay, 'side from being an asshole."

"Aren't we all?"

"Some more than others. Me a lot."

If my mother could let me be, reign in her threats and criticisms, we could get on with her book. Everything would be fine. I'd finish the memoir and return to my own writing, drafts and scribbles I had on tap. They'd been sitting on tap for how long now? I'd submerge myself in work and forget the fiasco with Catherine – after I helped Catherine move away. But to relocate an entombed body? To grave rob? Nothing I'd ever done, not even hiding Soames' body, matched the unorthodoxy of that.

My cellphone rang.

The house number.

"Yes?"

"You didn't go back to her house, did you?"

"You are fucking insane, mom."

"That doesn't answer my question."

"I'm not on a witness stand."

"Just tell me you're not at her house."

"I'm not at her house."

Silence.

"You believe me?"

"I don't want to call the police over this and tell them to go over there."

"I'm at the Fieldhouse Tavern. Having a drink."

I held up my phone and snapped a picture of the place — the bar counter, the red-topped stools, the two guys at the bar drinking bottled beer — and told her I'd send her the photo.

"Check your email," I said, and disconnected. If she called the police regardless, fearing a visual trick, that was on her back. A trip by a squad car to Catherine's house would anger the cops and embarrass my mother.

"Trouble with your girlfriend?"

Over their beers, the ponytailed guy and his friend were giving me self-satisfied looks.

"My...?"

"They mean Catherine," Tony said.

I'd forgotten these local barfly fuckwads had never gotten anywhere with Catherine, that they'd watched with envious wonder when I talked to her back in a booth. Hadn't they heard me use the word "mom"? Presumably not, but they'd have equal fodder for taunting if I said I'd been squabbling with my mother.

"What's the damage, Tony?"

"Sorry about your chick," the friend with the goatee said.

Despite the cold air outside, I still felt hot and headachy. I held the wheel tight and kept below the speed limit. Not that I get into bar fights, but I thought of the satisfaction I'd have felt punching those two losers' faces. Punching their faces and stomping on them. I had that image in my mind's eye when I turned my key and entered the house, and all I wanted right then was an unimpeded walk up the stairs to my room.

Get some sleep, forget this day ever happened.

But who has luck when they need it? My mother scooted out from the kitchen before I could cross the living room, and she asked me what I'd decided.

"About what?"

"The hospital. Is this going to be a fight?"

"It already is."

"I don't want to have to file papers, Kurt."

Were we caught in a loop? I darted past her and up the steps, running for my room.

She bounded after me.

"This is absurd."

"Then say yes."

We'd reached my room, where the light was still on.

"Can we discuss this in the morning? I don't feel well."

"It needs to be addressed now," she said.

"Everything with you is now now now. Fix this comma — now. Do this edit — now. Now's all I've heard from you for months."

"Attention to detail's important."

"The detail I need now is sleep."

"I'm afraid you'll wind up back at her house, harassing her."

"Unless I'm locked up."

"It's for rest and treatment."

"She's moving away so it's a moot point."

"But who'll be next?"

The pain in my head detonated, exploding with color, flaring to white, and I threw a punch at my mother's face. She tottered backwards across the floor and collided with my desk, scattering pages from the manuscript. That gave me an idea, which I put into effect: I snatched up and crumpled several pages and rammed the balled up mass at her mouth while gripping her neck with my free hand. Though dazed, she chopped at my arm, and I had to take the blows to keep my fingers on her throat. Papers in my fist, I punched her next in the forehead, and I saw her eyes roll up, consciousness leave. Her body sagged. I let her go and she collapsed in a heap. I kneeled, turned her over on her back, and sat on her chest. Thumbs to her windpipe, I squeezed and squeezed. Her thin neck was easy to choke. She lay with her limbs splayed out in the black and white track suit, and when her mouth fell open, all jaw tension gone, I stuffed the memoir pages in. I filled that maw till it could take no more.

Pretty? Not in the slightest. But I liked the headline the act evoked.

Memoirist made to eat her own words.

Book over, life over.

TWENTY-EIGHT

I didn't run. I didn't melt down. I engaged with the wine stash in my room, and at some point, in all my clothes except for my shoes, I passed out in bed. The second I opened my eyes, aware of daylight, morning, life and everything in it continuing, a hot flash shook my body and I felt liquids rise in my chest. Not from the hangover, though that was a lulu, but from the realization that I'd left my mother's body in the kitchen. To get her body out of my room, and needing a glass to drink the wine, I'd brought her down there last night and put her on the floor. I must've been thinking I'd return later and stick her someplace hidden – I couldn't recollect. I did know she lay on the kitchen floor this morning, and anyone who happened to look through the kitchen window would see her. What if someone came by, anyone, and saw? A million to one anyone would, but with the woebegone string I was on, this would be the day that happened. A driver with a flat in the road seeking help, the cops coming by bright and early to question me or my mother again about the night Ralph Soames disappeared.

I made it to the bathroom and spewed the liquids. My feet were bricks as I lumbered downstairs to confront her corpse. The heat inside me hadn't subsided, but the center of my being froze solid when I didn't see her body on the floor.

She wasn't in the kitchen.

I sat down at the table, my head in my hands.

We're inside. No dog could've come. It's not the woods.

Asshat.

From the clouds, the brain fog, a memory: drunk out of my gourd I'd been, but I'd lifted her body off the floor and carried it down to the basement sometime during the night. Before passing out? Must've been. And she was down in the basement now, secreted away.

No one knows. Stay calm.

I walked back upstairs to get the aspirin from my medicine cabinet.

TWENTY NINE

After coffee, breakfast, a shower, and a nap, when I felt sufficiently human again, I telephoned Catherine.

"I was supposed to call *you*," she said.

"Things have changed."

"How so?"

I told her, keeping it brief, and her response surprised me.

"This doesn't change anything."

"My mother's dead."

"Kurt, I'm leaving with June and we have a deal."

"Fuck our deal. My mother's dead. Your threat about telling her you have the book means nothing now."

"Is that why you killed her?"

"I don't follow."

"So I wouldn't have anything over you."

"Don't flatter yourself," I said. "But now that she's not around—"

"So you're going to renege?"

"I have a body here. That's what I'm thinking about."

I could use the woods for burial or her kiln downstairs for incineration. Yet digging another grave would be hideous and using the pottery kiln worse. The kiln wasn't human-sized and would entail dismemberment, feeding my mother to the oven piecemeal.

"I may have an idea," Catherine said.

"An idea for what?"

"Her body. Where to put it."

"Where?"

"Spare you lugging it into the woods like you did Soames."

"How thoughtful."

"Least I can do," Catherine said. "But after that, we're done. You help me with June, like we discussed, and I'll help you with your mother."

"Quid pro quo, huh?"

"I'll call you soon."

"I have a body here, Catherine."

"Put it on ice somewhere," she said. "Can't you do that?"

The coldest ice I know is your heart, I thought, and reminded her we were talking about my mother.

"Who you loved so much. Right."

"Doesn't anything upset you?"

"You've seen me upset, Kurt. What you did to your mother is your own craziness."

She told me she needed about a week, and then she'd be ready to get June and leave the area.

"I freed myself of my baggage," I said. "You can't do the same?"

"June's not baggage to me."

"Me without my mother. You without June. We could make that work."

Graveyard Love

"I'll call you in a few," she said, and broke off.

And when I had summoned the will to move, to keep on living despite everything, I carried my mother up from the basement and into the refrigerator room. The two massive fridges were there. It took rearranging, a shifting around of steaks and roasts, but she was lean enough to fit in a freezer.

THIRTY

Nobody likes rejection, and I was no different than anyone else. Help Catherine again and say farewell, nice knowing you? I'd reconsidered. I couldn't knuckle under so easily, and it was outrageous that in moving June from the vault to a casket to a truck that would take Catherine away, I would do the heavy lifting — literally. With her gone, I'd have nothing, not Catherine, not my mother's book, though I would have peace without my mother in the house. I'd have the time and solitude to get back into my own writing. Conversely, having given my utmost for the memoir, through sweat and quarrelling, anger and killing, I wanted to finish it. The book was ninety percent done and I could invent the rest. The voice throughout would be mine. No one would know where the truthful part ended and the fictional part began.

As for the author's disappearance:

She wrote it as her final testament. With death on her shoulder. A woman who had a fatal disease and made the decision to kill herself before the pain became all she had. She didn't want to rot away, in misery. But she got this finished. This book. Every word here is hers and this book is her story, her last offering to the world.

Would the public believe that? Would the police? Like with Soames, despite suspicions, investigators would have no body. And if I could get a death certificate somewhere, citing cremation, that she was in ashes…

One thing I knew beyond doubt: Catherine Embers had made a misstep. She never should have told me she had an idea about where to put my mother's body. I wouldn't have thought of that hiding place if she hadn't raised the topic, however allusively, but once I cottoned on to it, I acted. I did it late on a rainy night, and no one could have seen me do it.

Holed up inside, confident I had the advantage over Catherine, I waited for her call.

THIRTY-ONE

She came in a white panel truck, parking in the driveway. The night allowed for springtime weather, a turtleneck sweater on her, windbreaker jacket on me. Both of us wore gloves, though, and after Catherine opened the van's double doors, she climbed up into the back and grabbed one end of the box while I got a grip on the other. We lowered it to the ground. It was unvarnished and light, a beige wooden box with a hinged lid.

"Where'd you get this?"

"A carpenter guy in Kingston. Special order."

"It could pass for a storage chest. Doesn't even look like a coffin."

"That's the idea, Kurt."

"Clever."

Past the graveyard and over the hills hung a gauzy fog. Through the white tendrils, I could make out the moon, a wan sickle. A week of thunder showers had left the air moist, and the atmosphere felt charged, rife with electrical static, portending another storm.

"Let's get this done tonight," Catherine had said earlier. "Before it comes down again."

Catherine reached into the truck and put on a backpack. She closed the rear doors. She gave me a burlap sack in which she thought we would put June's body — protect it from bumping against the sides of the box as we carried it — and I flung the sack over my shoulder.

"We can leave the box here," I said.

"You sure?"

"She can't be heavy."

"But I thought—"

"Easier this way."

"I thought you'd want to handle her as little as possible."

"Dead bodies ain't much to me now," I said. "I've been handling them enough."

That got a split second smile from her and her voice even softened a note.

"It's almost over."

"For you," I said. "I still have my mother."

"One thing at a time. First June, then your mom."

I kept my poker face on, giving away nothing, and stretched my arm toward the road.

"Onward then."

She went, I followed, and I stared at her long red hair. It seemed eons ago that my madness for that color had first made me notice her making her regular visits to the graveyard. So much between us had happened since: crimes, fixations, and secrets had been shared, and yet here we were tonight, no closer as people than when we were strangers. Was there any other pattern? Why had I tried? The futility of my efforts saddened me, but I also felt a ripple of giddiness knowing what I had in store for her.

The mouth of the tomb was dark, inside the same. Catherine stopped. She swung one backpack strap off her shoulder, unzipped a compartment, and took out a green camping lantern. When she switched it on, its brightness made me squint, shield my eyes with my hand, but then I could see the entrance again and stepped with Catherine through the front room and into the room where the coffin lay.

It smelled of melted wax there, dead candles. The air was cooler than outside, cool and dry. The brass candle holders stood on the coffin, and Catherine didn't say anything about the holders looking out of place. I'd put them back on the coffin lid after my work the other night, and I thought that Catherine must've remembered that the candles had burnt out days ago, the time I brought her here after tasing her.

"You wanna open it, Kurt?"

She maneuvered behind me. I could feel her presence like a weight against my back. The lantern, which she held above my shoulder, made my ear hot and I felt perspiration on my cheek.

"What's wrong?" Catherine said. "Let's get it over with."

I bent to one knee and found the small hole in the floor. My thumb pressed the spring. With a clank, the coffin's lid activated, sliding back on its rollers, and what was inside became evident. Catherine edged forward, lantern by her face, hip touching mine now, and she peered down at the body with me. I heard her inhale and felt her stiffen. A croaking noise rose from her throat. I turned my head to look at her face and saw it had drained of blood. When her knees buckled, I thought she would swoon.

"You didn't think I'd figure what you meant? There's no better place to hide my mother."

After days in the freezer, she was partly defrosted, with the black and white sweat suit stuck to her purplish skin. I'd closed her eyes before freezing her and her expression looked restful. There were crystals in her white hair.

"Where's June?"

"She's safe."

"Where'd you put her?"

"I can show you"

"You disgusting prick."

"I'm not. But you'd go off with the love of your life and leave me here alone. It's not fair."

"What do you want, Kurt?"

"I want you to stay."

"And we'll get popcorn and be cuddly and watch horror movies together."

"Among other things."

"What was the one you raved about?"

"*Cat People*. Nineteen forty three. I'm telling you, it's a film you need to watch."

Something clanged and the light flickered — Catherine had dropped the lantern. She turned her back on me, hands out of my view, and brought one arm windmilling up. Before I could see what she had, a spray hissed in my face, and I felt an excruciating pain rack my eyes, as if they'd caught fire.

"Catherine!"

Blinded, fingers on my eyelids, I reeled backwards. The burlap sack fell off my shoulder. I sidswiped something, I think the coffin, and found myself falling. An electroshock hit me, stopping my heart, contracting my balls and entrails, and suck as I did, no air came. I felt an inability to move.

"Like the taser?"

Was I lying on the floor? Standing? Between the mace and the taser and the on-again off-again light, I didn't know whether I was up or down, and when something hard and heavy bashed my head, flight took hold.

I left the tomb, I soared.

In a tunnel of absolute darkness, I floated.

THIRTY-TWO

I became aware that my eyes had opened, but I continued to see blackness. There was no light anywhere, and no sound. I felt cold and a knot inside my head pulsed. Each surge of pain brought nausea. My eyes still burned but not too much and I could stand to keep them open. I lifted my arm to reach up and rub my eyes, but my hand struck a barrier. I pushed against it and found it unyielding. Trying with the other arm got the same result. I couldn't raise my arms more than a few inches before they hit this wall, nor could I flex my knees. A firm, flat surface pressed against one side of my body; along the other side, my right, was a soft clammy object. I twisted my neck and wrenched myself over as much as I could, and when my lips tasted hair, when my nose touched an ear, I knew.

That's when I screamed.

Where had Catherine gotten the strength? She wouldn't have needed to pick me up that far off the floor to cram me into the coffin, but it's not an act I would have thought she could do. She must've had the adrenaline flowing because of anger over my switch.

Sore loser, Catherine. We could've worked something out.

I stopped screaming.

Better to conserve my air.

Better to accept my predicament and hope that she came back.

But I knew she wouldn't.

Joke's on you. You'll never find where I put June.

I laughed at that, unable to contain myself, but my feeling of mirth didn't stick.

"You're awfully quiet, mom. No edits you want? No comments to make?"

That didn't perk me up either.

Around me, darkness and silence.

I took a long breath and screamed again.

ABOUT THE AUTHOR:

Scott Adlerberg grew up in the Bronx and a wooded suburb just outside New York City. His debut novel was the Martinique-set crime novel *Spiders and Flies*. His second novel, *Jungle Horses* was released last year from Broken River Books. His short fiction has appeared in various places including *Thuglit, All Due Respect,* and *Spinetingler Magazine.* Each summer, he hosts the Word for Word Reel Talks film commentary series in Manhattan. He lives in Brooklyn with his wife and two sons.

ACKNOWLEDGEMENTS:

Thanks to J David Osborne and Jeff Jackson for their helpful insight and advice as I was writing this book.

Made in United States
Orlando, FL
18 July 2025

63074138R10116